Sylvia's stallion was rearing up on its hind legs. Its front legs came crashing down just inches from where Jessie stood.

She scrambled quickly out of the way, but the stallion acted like an animal possessed. It continued to buck and kick.

For a brief moment, Jessie was concerned about Sylvia. The woman could be seriously hurt if she were thrown from the saddle. Even if she escaped injury in the fall, there was the very real danger of being trampled by the horse's hooves. Jessie dodged the horse, yet stayed as close as possible so that in the event Sylvia did fall, Jessie would be there to drag her to safety.

Then Jessie got a good look at Sylvia, and froze in anger. She expected to see a scared, helpless woman. Instead, she saw a calm, controlled rider with a face stretched into a cold, calculating grin.

◆─ WESLEY ELLIS ─◆

LONE STAR

AND THE
MONTANA LAND GRAB

J

JOVE BOOKS, NEW YORK

For Jason

LONE STAR AND THE MONTANA LAND GRAB

A Jove Book / published by arrangement with
the author

PRINTING HISTORY
Jove edition / December 1987

ISBN: 0-515-09328-9

Jove Books are published by The Berkley Publishing Group,
200 Madison Avenue, New York, New York 10016.
The name "JOVE" and the "J" logo
are trademarks belonging to Jove Publications, Inc.

PRINTED IN THE UNITED STATES OF AMERICA

10 9 8 7 6 5 4 3 2 1

Chapter 1

The two riders reined in at the edge of a low ridge. To the north the valley stretched out for as far as the eye could see. A long, broad alley matted deep with thick green grass shimmered as it stirred in the gentle spring breeze. Moving west the sea of green flowed into the foothills of the Sawtooth Mountains. The rocky peaks cut jaggedly into the clear blue sky.

Jessica Starbuck took it all in with a keen eye—a cattleman's eye which was trained to look at land and see the number of head it could support; and a woman's eye of cool green which noticed the beauty and peacefulness of the valley. She couldn't separate the two qualities that she observed in the valley; both were inherent parts of the land, just as they were inherent parts of the woman. Jessie, with her flowing mane of tawny blond hair, soft, satin-smooth skin and finely sculptured features, couldn't be anything but beautiful. But there was not only beauty, there was function. Anyone who had seen Jessie ride, rope, or shoot

1

could attest to it. That Jessie possessed grace, skill, and brains as well made her unique.

"A breathtaking stretch of land," she remarked.

Her companion, a tall, muscular man with shoulder-length black hair, nodded. He was half American, half Japanese. He was known as Ki, and was renowned as an expert martial artist. He was by nature and code a samurai. That his mixed parentage cost him his aristocratic position in the oriental land of his mother fortunately worked to the benefit of this western land, and specifically, of the Starbuck empire. Ki was a total samurai, pledged to Jessie.

He stared into the distance, eyes narrowing against the bright light. "With the sun just below the peaks, it reminds me of—"

"Mount Fuji," Jessie finished for him. She smiled when she saw his startled face. "Every mountain from the Canadian Rockies to the Tetons reminds you of Mount Fuji."

He nodded again, uninsulted by her playful jab. "They are all volcanic formations," he explained calmly, "as is Mount Fuji."

"Of course."

"And the image of Mount Fuji, well, it might have faded some," he added somewhat sheepishly.

"Really?" Jessie said questioningly.

Ki nodded. "I haven't seen Mount Fuji since I was a little boy."

"And how long ago was that?" Jessie asked with a smile.

"It was another world," Ki said simply.

"But how many years?" Jessie persisted. She didn't know how old Ki was, and though it was unimportant, she was curious as to his exact age.

Ki smiled. "Years?" He shrugged. "It was another time, another place."

2

"I don't know if you're afraid of me finding out how old you really are, or for that matter, how young you really are."

"Is there a difference?" Ki wondered aloud.

"One day, Ki, you'll latch on to the concept of vanity— or pride . . ."

"I have pride," Ki answered.

Jessie laughed. "You also have a sense of humor."

Ki laughed.

"But that doesn't answer my original question," Jessie continued.

"When I was a student we were taught to measure age not in years, but in experience."

"Let's go, oldtimer," Jessie said with just a trace of a smile. "I'd like to make the Box H by supper." With that she started her chestnut mare down the trail to the bottom of the valley. Ki brought his taller bay into step behind her.

"I think we're too late for dinner," Ki remarked dryly.

"What could have happened?" Jessie asked aloud as she surveyed the burnt remains of what was once the Box H ranch house. "Indians?"

Ki slid down from his horse, and started to poke through the charred timbers.

"There hasn't been any Indian trouble here since Chief Joseph surrendered," she said, answering her own question.

"I also don't think Indians use kerosene to burn down settlements." He kicked through the ashes and picked up a blackened tin container.

Jessie's voice faltered slightly. "Do you see any bodies?" She was afraid of the answer.

Ki thoroughly inspected the rubble before answering.

3

"No. The spread was probably abandoned before it was burned."

"That's curious."

"There are no animal corpses in the ashes of the barn, either."

"Why would the Hainleys pick up just like that?"

"I don't think we'll find an answer poking around here."

Jessie nodded. "Greenfield is at the north end of the valley. If we push, we'll make it by sundown."

The two horses kicked up a cloud of dust as they galloped down the wagon trail.

Greenfield was a small town, but it didn't lack any of the necessities; it just had fewer of them. There was one hotel, one saloon, one livery, one general store, and one boarding house of dubious repute. Jessie didn't attribute this to any unfair business practices. It wasn't so much business monopolies that kept competition out; rather it was the lack of clientele. The valley was settled mostly by ranchers. Cattle spreads, even small ones, tended to take up a lot of land. That meant there were a lot fewer people in the valley than one would suspect. If a store was well run, if the proprietor kept his customers satisfied, there was no need for another store. The trade couldn't support it. Same with a saloon. If the liquor wasn't too watered down, and the gambling tables not that crooked, one watering hole was enough.

Providing, of course, that the town wasn't solely owned by a single individual. There were towns, some smaller than Greenfield, some twice the size, that were owned and run by one man—who by virtue of excessive greed and ambition managed to get a stranglehold on the town's commerce. And it was never by honest competition and fair means by which he gained control.

Riding down the main street, Jessie didn't get that feeling about Greenfield. But it remained to be seen.

"Ki, why don't you get us a room in the hotel? I'll stop in the general store, and see if they can tell me anything about the Box H."

Ki nodded. "I'll wait for you in the hotel's dining room, if they have one."

Jessie dismounted outside the store and tied her horse to the rail. The sun had just set, and though it was after hours, there was a lamp on in the store. She tapped politely on the door, then turned the handle. The door opened.

"Hello. Anybody home?" she called loudly.

A tall, slightly built man emerged from the back of the store.

"I know it's late, but I saw the lamp burning," Jessie began.

The man smiled. "Stocking the new inventory," the merchant explained. "Run the store myself—me an' my wife. But with Betsy in the family way I work a little later to keep up with things."

"Well, congratulations, Mr. . . . ?"

"Newman, John Newman."

There was something in the tone of his voice, as well as his age, that made Jessie suspect it was his first. She asked and was proven right.

"Betsy wants a boy—she says it'll make things easier on me. But I'm so danged excited I'd be just as happy with a little filly."

"Good for you. I see no reason why a daughter couldn't help with the store."

Newman smiled. "But what can I do for you? I'm sure you didn't come in to hear about my family."

"I don't mind," Jessie said honestly. "But what I'd really like to hear about is the Hainleys and the Box H."

5

"You a friend of theirs, Miss . . ."

"Starbuck. Jessie Starbuck. I'm a friend, and a business associate. I run the Circle Star outfit out of Texas." Though the Starbuck name was well known, and most ranchers would have heard of the ranch, Jessie wasn't surprised that the name meant nothing to Newman.

The storekeeper nodded. "They picked up and moved on. Lock, stock, and barrel."

"Why?"

"Ain't no secret 'bout that. Turned out they didn't like working another man's land."

Jessie looked confused. "Josh Hainley owned the Box H—" she began.

"He owned a small parcel of land," Newman corrected. "Hardly worth breaking dirt over."

"I thought he was running a couple hundred head of cattle."

"He was."

"On an open range," Jessie concluded aloud.

"Leastways, he thought it was open range."

"But he found out to the contrary?" Jessie asked.

"That's right. Seems like most of the range the Box H cattle were grazing on was owned by an Eastern syndicate."

Jessie nodded. In essence she had gotten what she came for. "I reckon that answers my question, Mr. Newman. Much obliged." She started to leave.

"Anything else you need to know, feel free to ask," the merchant called after her.

Jessie stopped in the door and turned back to the storekeeper. "One last thing. How did Josh Hainley find out about this?"

"The Dobson Deed and Trust Company. They opened

an office right here in town, just a few months ago, it was."

Jessie had her answer, but she also had more questions. She brought them up over dinner. "Ki, Josh Hainley wasn't a tumbleweed operator. If he had a spread he'd have filed for the land. I'm sure of it."

"Sometimes men overlook the obvious."

"It doesn't sound like him," Jessie repeated.

"Open ranges are closing everywhere, Jessie. Soon they'll be a thing of the past. Like cap-and-ball pistols. If a man doesn't see the change coming he could be deceived."

"I don't like to see my friends chased off their land," Jessie said strongly.

Ki remained silent.

"I don't like to see hardworking, honest men cheated," she added.

"You never did, Jessie. But can we be sure Hainley was cheated and run off?"

Jessie started to speak, then changed her mind. After a moment's thought she answered, "No, but we can find out. First thing in the morning I'm waltzing over to the Dobson office."

"You may not get the answers you want,' Ki cautioned. "For that matter you may not get *any* answers."

Jessie was unflappable. "Eat your buffalo steak," she chided playfully.

Ki nodded. "You're right," he said seriously. "There won't be buffalo steaks on the table much longer either."

Morning came quietly to Greenfield. There was activity, but no thundering stagecoach, whistling train, or cussing mule team driver. The day began and the merchants opened shop. All save for the Dobson Deed Company.

Jessie waited on the boardwalk outside the office, at first very patiently, but as the minutes ticked away so did her patience. Eventually an adolescent boy came by to open up the office.

"I don't suppose you're the manager?" Jessie said with a smile.

The boy, sandy-haired and freckled, smiled back. "You'd be wanting Mr. McReedy. I'm just the runner here."

"When does Mister McReedy show up?"

The boy shrugged his shoulders. "There's no tellin', ma'am. He does a bit of travellin'. Recording, serving notice. He's all around the county."

"It's rather urgent," Jessie said. "Any idea where he might be?"

"Nope."

"Can you leave word for him that Jessica Starbuck would like to see him? I'm staying at the hotel."

"Sure thing, ma'am. But maybe I can help you."

"Maybe you can at that."

The boy straightened up. "I keep my ears open and my mouth shut," he said proudly.

"What's your name?" Jessie asked.

"Will. Will Grant."

"Well, Mr. Grant. Care to tell who's buying up land in these parts?"

"Gee, I . . ."

"Can you tell me what happened to the Hainleys and the Box H?"

"I know they pulled up stakes."

"But you don't know why?"

Will shook his head. "I was on my way to the county seat to record some deeds when it happened. When I got back, Hainley was gone."

8

"Thanks, Will."

The boy seemed disappointed that he couldn't be more of a help. Then he thought of something. "By the way, if it's any help, Mr. McReedy sometimes has to go to St. Jo."

"That might be of some use. Thanks again, Will."

"Sure thing, ma'am."

Jessie spent the rest of the morning making a few more inquiries. She could get nothing incriminating on either McReedy or the company he worked for. The general consensus was that the Dobson Deed Company was an evil necessity that came with progress. The oldtimers regretted seeing the county bought up by Eastern tenderfoots and their Eastern business interests, but accepted the fact that as the frontier opened and as the railroad branched out, outsiders were flocking in, some to settle, some to speculate. The wildness of the land was being tamed. Society, with its laws, regulations and money, quietly slipped in. It was a mixed blessing.

Jessie could ruminate on that for hours upon end. Often she would do just that while crossing the wide expanse of prairie. On long cattle drives she would sometimes slip into deep thought wondering what the future had in store. But right now she didn't have the luxury of idle thought. She wanted to know what happened to the Box H. The first step was to find and talk with McReedy.

She went back to the hotel and had a light afternoon meal with Ki. Afterwards she returned to the Dobson Deed company to find that not only was McReedy not there, but that Will was gone as well.

"Ki, the longer I wait the worse I feel about this whole thing," she said back in Ki's room.

"Pacing back and forth won't solve anything," he said gently.

"I'm open to suggestions."

Ki shrugged. "If the mountain won't come to you, go to the mountain."

"Exactly!" Jessie said with an excited smile, and rushed out.

Twenty minutes later she returned. "Let's go," she said to Ki.

"Where to?"

"The mountain. McReedy has a little cabin about two miles down the creek. We're going to pay a house call."

"I'll get the horses," Ki began.

Jessie shook her head. "They're saddled and waiting."

Ki slipped on his leather vest, automatically sliding his hand into the pocket to check that he had a ready supply of *shuriken,* the silver throwing stars that in his hands were as lethal as any revolver.

It appeared as if Jessie could read his mind. But it wasn't an act of clairvoyance that enabled Jessie to know his thoughts. After years of being together, the slightest gesture, the subtlest mannerism, conveyed his inner feelings. The look in Ki's eye could be read like a tabloid headline.

Jessie had to smile. "Ki, we're just going out to have a talk with the representative of Dobson Deed and Trust Company."

Ki remained silent.

Chapter 2

"That must be it," Jessie said as a small log cabin came in sight.

"Wait here, Jessie, and I'll go in and have a look."

Jessie frowned and started to argue. "There's no reason for all this caution, Ki."

Ki shrugged. It was an expression that said "better safe than sorry." Jessie had seen it many times before. Ki had often been proved right. His seemingly unnecessary caution had saved her life more than once.

Jessie resigned herself to the inevitable, but she had the last word. "Go ahead if you think there's a need," she said as she brought her horse to a stop.

As it turned out, there was a very real need.

Ki slid off his horse and handed the reins to Jessie. He had gone not ten yards more when the first shot rang out.

Dirt kicked up at his feet. Ki dove headfirst for the cover of a willow tree. He came up short by a few feet.

11

Another shot rang out and he flattened himself to the ground, giving as small a target as possible.

At the first crack of the gun, Jessie hopped off her horse and took cover in a slight gully. The depression kept her safely out of the line of fire, but she wasn't concerned about herself. She was worried about Ki lying out there in the open with a sniper taking a bead on him. It would be only a matter of time, likely seconds, before one of the shots hit the mark.

Jessie pulled out her Colt and started firing on the house. She kept her head low. It didn't matter if she hit something or if the shots were way off. All she wanted to do was give Ki a chance to make it to the willow tree.

After she'd emptied her revolver she took a fast look in Ki's direction. She didn't see him, and so she smiled. He must have made it.

The cabin was set in a field of grass a few yards from a gently flowing stream. There was no way to sneak up on it and no way to rush it. Its solid construction of logs was also sturdy enough to withstand prolonged assault. No .44 was going to pierce those walls of thick timber.

The man inside the cabin could keep Jessie and Ki pinned down for as long as he had ammunition. Jessie didn't want to guess just how long that could be. That left only one thing to do.

Cautiously Jessie raised her head. "Hold your fire!" she called out loudly. "We're here to talk."

In answer, a shot was fired from the cabin.

Jessie jerked her head down quickly, swearing to herself as she spit out some dirt. She wasn't about to give up. "McReedy, my name is Jessica Starbuck. I just want to have a few words with you," she yelled out, this time making sure to keep her head down.

12

There was no response. She took the lack of a gunshot as a positive sign and called out again.

"I'm a friend of Josh Hainley's. I'd like to know where he went."

From behind her she heard a soft thud. She turned quickly.

Ki smiled. "I'd save your breath."

"Ki!" She was obviously surprised to see him. "I thought you were tucked behind that tree."

"It was lonely there," he said with a grin. "I circled around."

"Do you think you can . . . ?"

Ki shook his head. "The cabin's out in the open. I'd be cut down before I made ten yards."

"You managed to make it here."

"It's one thing to retreat and another to advance," Ki explained simply.

Jessie knew he was right. "Then what do you think we should do?" she asked.

"I don't think we have much of a choice."

"That's a lot of help."

"We can't move in on the cabin, and we can't reason with him. That doesn't give us many more options."

Jessie didn't like the answer. She gave Ki a defiant look, then unbuckled her gunbelt. "McReedy," she called out loudly. "I'm coming out. Unarmed. I want to talk."

Slowly she raised herself up. She had barely gotten her head out from the gully when the rifle cracked and dirt shot in her face.

As she dropped back down, Ki offered her his bandanna.

"Don't be so smug," she snapped as she took the cloth and wiped the dirt from her eyes.

"It was a nice try, Jessie. It might have worked."

Jessie was not assuaged. "If you didn't, as a matter of course, go around pulling me out of tight spots, I could find myself getting very annoyed with you."

"We also learned something from your attempt at—"

"I learned not to get uppity," she interrupted.

"Besides that," Ki said with a smile.

"If you're going to give me another, 'I told you so, you should always listen to me' lecture, I think I'll stand up right this minute and take my chances against that rifle."

"We know that whoever is in there—"

"McReedy."

"Perhaps. But whoever it is isn't trying to kill you."

Jessie chuckled. "Well, he has me fooled."

"I think if he were trying to kill you, he would have waited till you presented an easy target."

Jessie nodded. "Another few seconds and I could have had a body full of lead, instead of a face full of dirt."

"I couldn't have said it better," Ki said with a grin.

Jessie looked thoughtful. "That presents an interesting situation."

Ki nodded. "I would say he's just trying to scare us off."

"We don't scare easily," Jessie said flatly.

"I know that. You know that." His head pointed towards the cabin. "But our friend in there . . . perhaps you'd like to tell him."

"Don't get smug." Jessie repeated.

Ki apologized. "I just wonder," he began a minute later. "Our friend in there seems to have been expecting company."

"You think he knew we were coming?"

"Maybe."

Jessie uttered one word. "Will."

"Who?"

14

"Will Grant, the office boy."

"Was he the only one who knew we had an interest in Mr. McReedy?"

Jessie shook her head. "John Newman. He told me where McReedy's place was. He had to know we were headed out here."

They both thought this over. "I also talked to half of the townspeople about either McReedy or the Dobson Company," Jessie added. "With any intelligence any of them could have put two and two together."

"And then again maybe whoever is shooting at us was expecting someone else."

"Like who?" Jessie didn't expect an answer; she asked the question automatically.

Ki shrugged. "About the only thing I'm sure of is that things aren't totally aboveboard."

Jessie agreed. "Honest agents of honest deed companies don't shoot when people start getting a little nosy."

Ki smiled. "Once again your intuition proves correct." His face then stretched into a broad grin. "But if you're going to give me one of your 'I told you so' lectures, I'm going to hop right up and rush that cabin."

Time passed slowly. Periodically Jessie would raise up and fire a few shots at the cabin. They were always answered. Eventually she grew tired of the game, and with a heavy sigh lay down to wait it out.

"The sun should be setting soon, Jessie," Ki remarked. "It will get dark quickly once it dips below those mountains."

"I reckon I can wait that long to give our Mr. McReedy a piece of my mind."

"I wouldn't want to miss that," Ki said with a laugh.

"You won't."

15

"I don't know."

"As soon as the light goes I'm going to pump a heap of lead into that cabin. And I'm not going to stop till you give the word—from inside."

"A good plan, but . . ."

Jessie looked skeptical. "Are you trying to tell me, Ki, that under the cover of darkness, with me firing continuously, you won't be able to sneak around back and get the drop on McReedy?"

"I'll sneak all right, but getting the drop may prove difficult."

"I bet." She sounded sarcastic. "He'd have to be a lot more man than the average deed recorder. In fact he'd have to be a hell of a man. Two or three more than likely."

Ki smiled. "Thank you for the vote of confidence . . ."

Jessie snorted at his modesty.

Ki continued. "But it's hard to get the drop on a phantom."

"And what's that supposed to mean?" Jessie asked.

"McReedy may want us cowering in this gully all day, or he may just keep us pinned here till he can effect his getaway."

"That's a good point," Jessie agreed. "It may call for a change in the basic plan."

"When you've come up with it, let me know."

It was nearly dark, and Jessie had not formulated a new plan. She pulled out her Colt, a beautiful slate-gray revolver with a polished peachwood grip that fit her hand perfectly. The gun was a custom-made .38 on a .44 frame. It was lighter and packed less recoil than the standard Colt Peacemaker. But her deadly accuracy with the weapon more than made up for the diminished size of the cartridges. She broke open the revolver and reloaded the three empty chambers. With a quick flick of the wrist the revolver snapped shut.

"Ready?" Jessie asked.

"It's not that I'm shirking my responsibility, Jessie, but why not try a test shot or two."

Jessie raised her gun and fired two shots. They were answered almost immediately. She turned to Ki. "Satisfied?" she said with a grin.

"It was just a suggestion," Ki answered. "Now I know, and I'll take proper precautions."

Jessie nodded. "Try not to get shot." The words were facetious, but the emotion was not.

"Don't worry," Ki assured her. "There are enough shadows to conceal my movements. It will take me a few minutes, but I'll ge there." He squatted down on his haunches. "Any time you're ready, Jessie."

Jessie raised her head and opened fire on the cabin.

She didn't hear Ki leave the gully, but she knew he was already on his way. He was right about the visibility. Even though she knew he was out there she couldn't spot him. She emptied her gun, quickly reloaded, and continued pumping lead into the cabin.

It crossed her mind that this time there was no return fire, but she didn't pause to think about it. She just fired, reloaded, and fired some more.

For Ki, a master in the art of stealth, the crawl towards the cabin did not represent the slightest danger. Considering the lack of light even a layman, if he moved carefully and slowly, could have reached the cabin. But Ki was cautious only for the first few yards. The initial movement, the climbing out from the gully, was the only point at which Ki could have been spotted. But Jessie took care of that. Her quick fire would have forced McReedy's head down.

Those few seconds were all that Ki needed. By the time Jessie had to reload, by the time McReedy had a chance to peer out from the cabin, Ki was already yards away, moving like a snake through the grass. Ki ran the same risk as a diamondback of being spotted—slim at best.

He soon had the cabin flanked. Out of sight from the front window, he rose to his feet and raced to the side of the building.

He paused and listened. For a moment he thought he heard something. Then Jessie's revolver started barking, and the faint sound, real or imagined, was blotted out.

Ki turned the back corner. He expected to find a window but instead, tacked on to the rear wall of the cabin, there was a small shed, just big enough to shelter two horses, or, if one lived alone, a horse and a pair of hogs.

That didn't change the plan. Chances were good that there was a door connecting the shed to the house. Silently he started towards the shed, then stopped short. He did hear a sound. The house partially blocked out the noise of Jessie's gunfire, and Ki could clearly hear some rustling coming from within the shed.

It was probably the horse fidgeting, spooked by the gunfire. Nothing more. Still, Ki moved cautiously. There was no assurance that it was the horse. And unless Ki knew something to be definite, unless he could be certain, he always left room for the unexpected. Mentally and physically, he was alert and ready as he inched around the edge of the shed.

He was still taken by surprise.

Had he not been primed, had he been even slightly off his guard, he would have been trampled by the large roan that came bolting out of the shed.

Quickly Ki dove backwards. As he flew through the air his head led the way, but before he hit the ground his legs flipped over and landed first—a smooth backwards flip. Ki stood on his feet.

His hand went into his vest pocket, but by the time he pulled out one of his throwing stars the horse and rider were racing off out of range. That's not to say Ki couldn't, in a matter of life or death, bring down the rider. He could. In fact he could hurl the *shuriken* twice that far. But as the distance increased the accuracy diminished. Especially with a moving target, he couldn't guarantee the point of impact. Ki couldn't take the chance of the *shuriken* striking the rider in the base of the head or neck. A wound like that would instantly kill.

The last thing he wanted was to kill the rider. He wanted to know who was shooting at them, and why. Dead men were infamous for being tight-lipped.

Jessie paused a moment. Then she heard it, definitely.

"Hold fire!" It was Ki calling out from the cabin.

She holstered her Colt and climbed out of the gully. She was surprised when the door opened and Ki stepped out— alone.

"Where's McReedy?" she asked as soon as she reached Ki.

"Gone. He took off on horseback."

"Damn!"

"I barely missed him," Ki added quite literally.

"I guess you were right about that," Jessie conceded.

"I would much rather have been wrong," he said in all seriousness.

Jessie nodded. "Let's round up our horses. If they haven't strayed too far he won't have much of lead on us." She started for the door.

"There's no hurry," Ki said calmly.

"I don't want that skunk to slip away."

19

"Neither do I, but it's dark. We're unfamiliar with the terrain. McReedy, or whoever, isn't."

"I wish you'd stop it," Jessie said peevishly. "That was McReedy."

"We don't know that."

"I do!" A moment later Jessie's voice softened. "I'm sorry for snapping. I don't like being holed up all afternoon only to let our man slip away."

"He won't get away, Jessie. I only said there's no hurry. I suggest we get our horses, go back to the hotel, and get a good meal and a good night's sleep."

"I reckon so." She sounded defeated.

"Besides, this could turn out to be a real chase. We don't have bedrolls, food, or extra ammo. We're ill prepared to mount an extensive trail."

Jessie nodded. "Ki, I hate to think that without you I might do something foolish and half-cocked."

"I doubt that," he said seriously. "An hour from now, when you lost sign, you'd head back and start out fresh tomorrow. This way we just get to eat a little earlier."

"And I gather you've worked up quite an appetite lying on your back all day in that gully."

"Quite," he agreed.

"Ki," she began exasperatedly, "I've seen you go for days without food."

"True."

"Then how can—"

"A mule can go days without food too, but that doesn't mean he won't eat when he can."

Jessie looked him straight in the eye. "You're absolutely right. I've never noticed the similarity before."

"Are you saying I'm muleheaded?"

Jessie smiled. "Some folks incorrectly call them asses."

Chapter 3

Jessie and Ki returned to the hotel, where they both had a heaping portion of beef stew, the special of the day. They ate in silence, then retired to their rooms.

Jessie was tired but even after she doused the lamp and closed her eyes, her mind continued to race.

Originally, she had only wanted to talk to someone from the Dobson Deed Company. But today's incident out at the cabin changed all that. It was clear her business with them now involved more than simple chit-chat.

She tried to figure out why McReedy had fired upon them, but could come up with no satisfactory answer. That would have to wait till they caught up with him.

Jessie stared out the window at the crescent moon, which hung low in the sky. With McReedy putting more miles between them every minute, sunup was a long way off, and too slow in coming.

There was nothing Jessie could do about it but try to sleep. In the next day or two they would have to make up as much time as possible. Jessie knew she should get her sleep while she could. Many nights might pass before she would find herself lying in a bed enjoying the luxury of clean sheets.

She chuckled at the thought. In truth she was every bit as comfortable in a bedroll under the stars as she was in a fancy bedroom. Maybe even more so.

Nothing could compare to the cool feel of a gentle night breeze. And every region, from the mountains to the desert, had a smell of its own. Whether it was the grama grass of Texas, the sagebrush of the plains, or the pine needles of the timberland, Jessie always liked to lie under the stars and breathe in the fragrance that drifted in on the night air. All the quilted mattresses and all the goose-down pillows in the fine bedrooms of the world couldn't measure up to that.

Still, Jessie needed to get some rest. Staying awake the whole night would not solve any problems. It wouldn't make McReedy any easier to track. It wouldn't make the dawn come any sooner; it would only make her eyes heavy and tired when it did come.

She turned on her side, and with a heavy sigh, forced herself to sleep.

Ki also found it difficult to sleep. He too had many questions running through his head. But he did not push them aside. He got up from his bed and acted.

He went to the general store, where, without much to-do, he slid in through a rear window. Inside he took a chance and lit a lamp. If anyone happened to pass by, the faint light of a match might stir up some interest, whereas a passerby might take the lamp as nothing more than the proprietor working late. Besides, he wouldn't be long.

Ki didn't find any dynamite. It was just as well. The

22

sticks of explosives were a little too powerful for his needs. Another minute of looking and he found something that suited his purposes even better. He grabbed three gunny-sacks, filled them with a mixture of saltpeter, sulfur, and charcoal, then tied them tight with strong twine.

He left the way he had come.

Ki walked quickly down the street. Then, ducking into a side alley, he came upon the rear of the Dobson Deed and Trust Company. He jimmied open a side window and climbed in.

He was feeling his way around, looking for a lamp, but there was none where he expected one. He was about to strike a match when he heard a stirring.

"Chase, that you?" someone called out from the rear of the store.

Ki thought about taking flight, but that would serve no purpose. The other possibility, to remain in the dark and try to avoid detection, became impossible as the glow of an oil lamp filled the back room and spilled out into the office.

The light grew brighter as it was carried into the office by a startled young man. "You're not Mr. McReedy," he blurted out needlessly.

Ki agreed, "No, I'm not."

"Then what are you doing here?" the young man de-manded to know.

"I'm looking for McReedy," Ki lied. "What are you doing here?"

"I'm waiting for him. He told me not to leave till he showed up."

Ki's eyes adjusted to the brightness of the lamp. Not only could he see much better but he could see that the other person in the room with him was only a boy, tall for his age, but no more than fifteen. He smiled. "You must be Will."

The boy started to nod, then his eyes grew suspicious. "I don't recall seeing you around here afore." One hand slipped to his back pants pocket and drew out a bowie knife. "You'd best tell me what you want. I may look young, but I know how to use this."

Ki didn't doubt it. But he didn't look too scared.

Will noticed and added somewhat nervously, "Don't make me prove it."

"I hope it won't come to that," Ki said. "But I think it might be a good idea to set that lamp aside."

The boy did not move.

"I don't think you'll be able to use that knife too effectively with the lamp in your other hand."

Will realized the truth in that and put the lamp down on the desk.

What Ki failed to mention was that as soon as the oil lamp was safely out of the way he would be free to strike. Getting the knife away from the boy would be easy; making sure the lamp wouldn't drop and start a fire was something else entirely.

Will had scarcely let go of the lamp before Ki was upon him.

The boy reacted quickly and skillfully, but he was no match for a trained martial artist.

As soon as Ki moved in, Will jabbed with the blade. But Ki's hands were quicker. His right hand caught the boy's wrist in a firm grasp. His left took hold of Will's hand and squeezed hard. Ki pivoted, stuck his hip out, and flipped the boy over. Before Will hit the ground the bowie knife was in Ki's grasp.

Will look stunned. He lay there and rubbed his sore hand.

"I'm sorry I had to do that," Ki said.

"What do you want?" Will asked again. But this time there was fear in his voice.

"I don't want to hurt you," Ki assured him. "I just want to have a look at some papers."

Will studied him curiously.

"If McReedy had been in today, this wouldn't be necessary. But I don't know when he'll be back, and I can't wait."

Some of the fear had gone from Will's eyes.

"I don't even have a gun," Ki said with a smile.

Will laughed and pulled himself up. "I don't reckon you need one at that."

Ki smiled. "You'll be more comfortable in that chair."

Will took it as an order and did what he was told.

Ki searched quickly through the office cabinets but found nothing of any interest. Certainly nothing that would explain why the Hainleys had been kicked off their land, or why McReedy had used Jessie and himself for target practice. But he didn't expect to find anything there. Anything of importance, and he deemed something that would cause a shootout important, would be locked in the safe. That was why he had stopped off first at the general store. But perhaps there was a simpler way.

He turned to Will. "I want to have a look in the safe."

"I can't do that."

"I don't want to hurt you . . ." Ki began a threat he had no intention of carrying out. But Will could not know that.

Will shook his head quickly. "I mean I can't open the safe. I don't have the combination."

Ki believed him. "Take off your shirt," he ordered, as he tucked the knife into his waistband.

Will did so.

"Now put your hands behind your back," Ki said as he picked up the shirt.

Using the shirt he tied the boy's hands. "I'm not going to bother gagging you," he explained. "If you yell for help I'll be the first one in here. Likewise, if I return and I don't find you sitting right where I left you . . ."

"Don't worry, I ain't moving," Will promised. "I ain't making a peep."

"Good."

Ki unlocked the front door and hurried to the other end of the town.

Out past the last building of Main Street he stopped and took out two of his gunnysacks. Using the knife he cut off three pieces of twine from the extra that was wrapped around the sacks. Two were identical in length; the other was considerably longer. Then he made a small incision into the sacks and stuck the long piece of rope into one. He placed it on the ground then, inserting the next piece of twine into the other sack, and placed it exactly the length of its string away from the first sack.

Ki struck a match and lit the long rope.

He got up and ran back to the Dobson Deed Company.

Inside the office, Ki knelt down at the safe and placed the last remaining gunnysack on the handle of the lock. He punctured the cloth and inserted the last piece of string.

It was a makeshift setup. Many things could go wrong. But Ki had enough experience with explosives of his own making to trust things to work out. In his mother's land of Japan, a working knowledge of explosives was an essential part of a master warrior's training. There, *nage teppo*— small bombs—were used by the *ninja*—professional assassins—for any number of purposes. There were bombs designed for loud noises, smoke, blinding light, and of course, explosive wallop. After learning how to make and use *nage teppo,* the small explosive necessary to blow open a safe presented little difficulty.

All that had to happen was the first fuse had to burn completely and ignite the first explosion, which in turn would light the second fuse, which would also burn completely to explode the second sack. At the first explosion, Ki would light his fuse in the office, which would burn for the same amount of time as the fuse at the other end of town. The explosion at that end of town would mask the sound of the explosion in the office. Simple. Despite everything that could go wrong, it could work.

In fact, it did.

The plan worked so well, it was even more of a disappointment that it availed nothing.

The safe did not hold any incriminating evidence. It contained nothing to link the Dobson Company with any wrongdoing. It held nothing illegal in it. In fact, it was completely and absolutely empty.

Ki waited the rest of the night in the office. McReedy had told the boy to wait for him till he returned. Perhaps McReedy was coming back. It was a long shot but Ki had nothing better to go on. With Will, he waited it out.

By the first signs of dawn Ki realized McReedy was long gone. The boy had only been instructed to wait in order to throw them, or someone, off the trail. McReedy had no intention of returning.

Eager to get started, Jessie awoke before the dawn. She got dressed quickly and headed downstairs. The hotel cook was just firing up the large iron cookstove. He was more than happy to put up a pot of coffee and warm some biscuits and ham.

After a short wait she took her cup of coffee and stepped outside to watch the first crack of light spread across the sky. It was still cool, but the clear sky and bright streak of

27

orange that was stretched across the horizon promised a scorcher of a day. They would have to pack extra water.

Jessie then noticed a lamp burning in the general store. She nodded. A hard worker like John Newman would be an early riser.

She walked over there and asked the merchant to fill an order for her. He was happy to oblige.

Jessie smiled to herself as she left for the livery. By the time Ki woke up, breakfast would be waiting and their horses would be saddled and packed.

She had gone only a few steps when her smile first faded from her lips. Then it grew even wider.

Coming from the other side of town was Ki, and he was leading their two mounts.

"I thought you were still sound asleep," Jessie said as they met in the middle of the street.

"Great minds think alike," he said with a grin of his own. "I was just wondering how long to let you sleep."

"Ki, you know better than that," she chided playfully. "I don't want you to let me sleep at all."

"A few minutes never matter, Jessie."

"A few minutes can sometimes make an important difference."

"True, but you're so hard to wake."

"Now that's not true! I'll wake at the slightest disturbance. I pop up ready and alert. Almost as fast as you, Ki."

Ki smiled. "I meant you look so peaceful when you sleep, you're hard to wake. Very angelic," he added.

"Oh," she said simply, not knowing exactly how to respond. "Are you saying I don't look peaceful and angelic when I'm awake?" she demanded to know a moment later.

The smile remained on Ki's face. "Let's just say the cougar in you comes alive."

"I'll take that as a compliment," she snapped.

"By all means." He paused a moment, then continued. "I find it hard to believe no one has ever told you that you have the look, the cunning, and the ferocity of a mountain lion."

"I reckon they're all afraid of my bite. Speaking of which, the cook has biscuits and hot coffee waiting. I've had mine," she said as she took hold of the horses' reins. "Go grab yourself some; you look like you could use it. I'll be loading up at the general store."

"While you're at it, pay for three sacks of gunpowder."

"I thought I heard something last night."

Ki smiled. "It was only a minor explosion. I hope it didn't disturb your sleep," he teased.

"You're playing with fire, Ki."

"Don't I know that."

"A mountain lion can strike at any moment."

"I think I'll grab that cup of coffee now," he said with a smile. He walked quickly towards the hotel.

The trail was not hard to pick up. In the soft grassland it was easy to cut for sign. It started at McReedy's cabin and headed due west. Understandably, with McReedy hitting the trail at night, his main concern was putting distance between himself and his would-be pursuers.

A few hours later they found the spot where McReedy stopped. Whether he spent the night there or only a few minutes to rest his horse could not be determined. Jessie and Ki pushed on. Until they could get some idea of how far behind they were they weren't going to stop. They didn't overwork their horses, but continued steadily on, eating, drinking, resting in the saddle.

By late afternoon, the rich grassland was thinning out. It was still good grazing, but the ground was drier and rockier, making it harder to cut for sign. A few times Jessie had to lean over the neck of her horse to study the ground.

McReedy was still moving west. He was traveling in an almost straight line and seemed unconcerned about covering his tracks. Perhaps he didn't expect pursuit.

Another two hours later, Jessie began to realize what was in McReedy's mind. "He seems to know exactly what he's doing," Jessie remarked.

Ki nodded. "Tough terrain to cut for sign."

"That's why he didn't care about leaving us an easy trail. He could make a straight dash for it and hope to lose us in the badlands."

The valley they had been in seemed to stretch all the way to the mountains, but now as they stood on the edge of it they could see that in between were miles of dry, craggy, baked badlands. Even if they managed to track McReedy through that, there were probably a dozen streams feeding down the mountain that could completely wash out a trail.

Ki remained optimistic. "Of course, McReedy doesn't know he has you trailing him."

"You think he'll get careless?"

"Most trackers would probably turn back about now. If not, then by the next day."

"I'm not most trackers," Jessie said firmly.

Ki laughed. "Time and terrain are on his side, but we have the advantage."

Jessie looked at him questioningly.

"We have you," he said simply.

"We won't lose him," Jessie promised. "But it will make the going slow."

"I think he'll slow his pace some too."

"Well, let's push on."

"Why don't we pack it in for the day?" Ki suggested.

"There's still a few hours of light," Jessie protested.

"Two at best. That won't take us far. And I was think-ing of the horses. There's better grazing here, and we passed a small creek about a half-mile back. Who knows what we'll find up ahead?"

"We're packing enough water, and some oats," Jessie began.

"Who knows what's up ahead?" Ki repeated. "We're assuming he's heading for the mountains. But what if he turns south into the desert?"

Jessie nodded. "I reckon we've done enough for one day. Another few miles won't matter at all. Let's go find that stream. I could use a cold soak."

Chapter 4

Staying on McReedy's trail turned out to be slow, painstaking work. Every few yards Jessie had to dismount and check the ground for sign—a chipped rock, a dislodged stone, a faint hoofprint. But she kept at it. And as promised, she did not lose the trail.

Jessie was an expert tracker. Ki could tell; he was one himself. He had acquired his skill with cold logic, raw intellect, and a seasoned eye. Ki knew what to look for and knew how to read what he found. He could see a print and from the erosion of the imprint tell its age. He could look at the spacing of the prints and tell if the animal was walking, running or stalking. Many times he would inspect a track and tell a whole story about the animal that left it. The stories turned out to be amazingly accurate. But even with all his skill, he might have lost McReedy's trail. He was quick to admit that were it not for Jessie, they might be wasting hours running around in circles.

Jessie had something that Ki considered beyond skill.

Some might call it a knack. Sometimes it seemed she just played a good hunch, but she did it all too frequently for it to be regarded as luck. Ki knew it was an art.

Jessie had an inner sense, a feeling that put her on the right track and kept her there. She knew enough not to question it. Ki certainly wouldn't. Therefore he readily agreed when Jessie suggested a change in tactics.

"Ki, we're not getting anywhere," she began. "We haven't lost him, but we're making such bad time, it's almost pointless."

"At least we haven't lost him."

"Ki, by the time we make it out of these badlands the trail could be so cold it'd be about the same as if we had lost him."

"Unless I don't know you, I'd say you're hinting at an idea."

Jessie smiled. "Once, just once, I'd like to have the feeling that you don't know what I'm going to say before I say it."

"Jessie, if I didn't understand you somewhat, all these years together would have been a terrible waste."

Jessie chuckled. "Like knowing how your favorite horse is going to react."

"Something like that," Ki agreed.

"Well, then I can assume you don't mind if we chuck prudence to the wind and kick up some dust."

"If that's what you suggest," he answered plainly.

Jessie nodded. "McReedy's not heading for the mountains, but he's clearly following the chain south. My guess is he's trying to circle around them."

"He could just be heading south," Ki suggested.

"Maybe. But then why is he always staying about a half-day's ride from the mountains?" Jessie didn't wait for an answer. "I think he's sticking to the badlands to lose us, but he plans on heading west, either through a cut in the mountains, or by flanking them on the south."

"It's possible."

"I think we should ride hard for the rest of the day. Before dusk we'll stop and I'll cut for sign. Even if we have to do it afoot, we'll make up lots of time."

"It's worth the chance," Ki said.

"I don't think it's much of a gamble. If he's heading for a pass there should be enough sign—if not in fact a clear trail for us to pick up. And if there isn't, we'll just keep the mountains on our right. We'll find something eventually."

Ki nodded.

Jessie nudged her horse into a gallop. Ki was right behind.

The plan did not work as well as expected. By sundown, Jessie was on her hands and knees cutting for sign. But she found nothing.

Over a meal of beans and jerky, Jessie admitted she might have made a mistake.

"I don't think so," Ki said.

"And why do you sound so sure?" Jessie wanted to know.

"I thought I saw smoke out there," he said nonchalantly.

"When? Where?" Jessie asked excitedly.

"Now don't get excited, I can't be certain."

"Ki, I have never known you to make a statement you weren't positive about."

"Now who's the expert on my behavior?" he said playfully.

"It comes from years of knowing you," she said with only a trace of humor. "When did you spot it?"

"It was only the faintest wisp. It might have been the heat or—"

"Ki! When?"

He no longer evaded the question. "While you were studying the ground, a little ways back. Just before we stopped."

"Why didn't you say something before?" she asked quickly. "How far off? Can we make it tonight?"

"That's exactly why I didn't say anything. If it was McReedy's smoke, he's still quite a ways off."

"We have all night."

"We need to give the horses a rest. We've been running them hard all afternoon."

Jessie seemed unconvinced.

"But I don't think we'd make it by sunup anyway. There's no point riding all night and winding the horses."

"I suppose another day of hard riding will accomplish near the same thing," Jessie admitted grudgingly.

Ki nodded. "Now get some sleep."

They were back in the saddle by dawn.

It was a day of hard riding, but by late afternoon they found their first reward—a small ring of burnt ashes.

"Looks like it was just enough to heat a cup of coffee," Ki remarked as he looked down at the remains of the fire.

"I can't decide if that means that McReedy suspects we're still trailing him, or if it's a sign that he thinks we've given up and turned back."

Ki smiled. "He probably can't decide himself."

"A cup of coffee instead of a hot meal? On the slim chance we're still tracking him?"

"Exactly."

"Well I'd hate for McReedy to pass up a hot meal for nothing," Jessie remarked as she pointed her bay after her quarry.

* * *

The rest of the day went fast. Jessie was able to keep a good pace without losing sign.

They rode well into the day, stopping much later than they had the day before. In fact the sun had already set by the time they made camp. But after another cold meal, Jessie was anything but tired.

"Ki, the moon is fairly bright and the horses haven't been pushed too much today. . . ."

Ki stood up, picking his saddle up with him. There was no need for Jessie to finish her sentence. "Only a few more hours, Jessie. Don't even think about riding through the night."

Jessie was satisfied. "A few hours is all I'm asking for."

The moon gave just enough light to check for sign. Here the flat, hard dirt was a help. In thick grassland the shadows would have made it very difficult to trail at night. In timber country it would have been impossible.

Both Jessie and Ki lost track of the time, but it must have been well after midnight when Ki caught Jessie dozing in the saddle.

It was not an uncommon or dangerous thing to do. On cattle drives it was fairly common. Many a trail boss would get little sleep save for what he could get in the saddle.

But pushing four thousand head of cattle and stalking a would-be killer entailed different risks. Ki did not want Jessie tired and bleary-eyed when they caught up with McReedy.

He watched Jessie closely till he saw her stir in the saddle. "I think it's time to pack it in," he said gently.

Jessie sat up straight. She realized she had been dozing. There was no shame it. On the contrary. Only an experienced rider could sleep in the saddle; only an expert would dare it.

She smiled at Ki. "I reckon I got my hour's worth."

"I'll take care of the horses, Jessie. You lay out your bedroll."

Jessie didn't protest.

She was asleep the moment her head hit the ground.

When Jessie awoke Ki already had the horses saddled and the bags packed. She smiled to herself. It was just like Ki to let her sleep those extra minutes. But she had to admit that after the last two days she really needed the rest. The sun had risen and was beginning to take the chill out of the night air, and as she crawled from her bedroll she felt a strange exhilaration. The air was clean and brisk, but it was more than that. She was alert yet relaxed, tense but calm. A coiled copperhead came to mind, in that deadly repose the moment before it strikes, lightning-quick. And after days on the trail they too were close, close to striking.

"Good morning." Ki smiled and handed her a steaming cup of coffee. "I think it's time you had a hot cup of coffee," Ki explained. "It's dry wood, very little smoke."

Jessie shook her head. "It's getting late. You should have woken me."

"A few minutes won't matter. We'll catch up with McReedy before sundown."

Jessie took the cup, her fingers curling around its warmth. ·

"And when you're finished," continued Ki, "there's some water warming to freshen up with."

Jessie smiled again. But she realized Ki was not just being considerate. Ki rarely did anything for just the obvious reasons. There was an underlying edge to even this simple act of hospitality. It would be a grueling ride across

37

dry, open terrain, and there could be a lot of lead to pump before the sun would set. Relaxed moments would be few and far between.

The day was like the other two, but oddly enough Jessie felt the effects of the terrain and the weather more this day. Perhaps it was that her mind was free of worry. It was no longer a question of whether they would catch McReedy or not. It was now only a matter of time, of hours. Or perhaps it was the accumulation of the days, the cumulative effect of two days' hard riding through rough terrain. Or maybe it was much simpler. Maybe the day was just hotter than the others.

The afternoon sun beat down on their backs as Jessie and Ki continued through the badlands. The constant blinding glare reflecting off stone and dirt alike was as bad as the heat. Were it not for the large brim of Jessie's gray Stetson, her eyes and fair skin would be easy prey for the sun's searing rays. Jessie undid the canteen from her saddle horn, and moistened the red bandanna that was tied around her neck. The wet cloth felt cool and refreshing against her hot skin. She took a sip, then handed the canteen to Ki.

It was a subtle change that was not easily noticed, but since morning the land had been dropping in elevation. They were moving slowly into a large, round basin. The change in the ground underfoot caught Jessie's attention. It was baked hard as adobe. More importantly, for the last half-mile there had been no trace of their quarry. No print, no sign.

Jessie pivoted in her saddle, worried for the first time. "Do you think we lost him, Ki?"

"Perhaps."

"He knows the land. He knows that once in this basin he could lose us cold."

"Perhaps," Ki repeated. "But I think you were right all along." He reined his horse to the right. "The mountain range we've been following tapers off dead ahead. My guess is that he's heading straight for those foothills." Ki pointed to the gently rising bluffs that lay a few miles due west.

"I think so, too." Jessie suddenly reined her horse to a stop and swung down effortlessly from the saddle. Bending down she picked up a discarded half-smoked butt.

"I'd say that's a pretty convincing sign," Jessie said, smiling. "And an awful interesting coincidence . . ." Her smile slowly faded. She scratched her mare's velvet-smooth nose and pondered a moment before climbing back into the saddle. She gently prodded the horse forward, her soft green eyes narrowing sharply as she studied the far horizon. As Ki watched her, a slight smile formed on his handsome face. Suddenly Jessie turned to him.

"Ki, are you thinking what I'm thinking?" she asked abruptly.

"The butt was no coincidence." It was neither question nor answer.

Jessie continued, "The ground was hard, there were no prints and just when I was afraid I'd lost him—this . . ." She held up the butt. Ki nodded. Thinking out loud, she went on. "It's as if he was leaving markers, like he wanted us to follow. It might be a trap."

Ki turned to her and simply stated what was obvious to one trained in the ancient Japanese art of *bushido*, "the way of the warrior." He spoke with an assurance that Jessie had come to trust and respect. "A trap discovered is no trap at all."

Unconsciously, Jessie shifted her gunbelt forward. Her revolver looked right at home against her rounded hip. She straightened in the saddle and spurred the mare into a gallop.

They reached the foothills in the late afternoon, and as Ki predicted, by sundown they were crouched behind a boulder looking down at a small palomino tethered to the side of a cabin. The cabin was small and plain, probably built by some prospector or trapper as a way station before crossing the wide expanse of badlands. It was set in the basin of three surrounding hills, and unless one knew of its location, it could remain undetected. If it were not for the thin column of light gray smoke streaming out of the stovepipe, Jessie and Ki might have missed it altogether.

"Jessie, I'm going to circle the cabin and make sure there are no surprises."

"'Cepting us." Jessie showed her white teeth, though it was more a snarl than a smile.

"Right," Ki answered, then slipped off to the next boulder, his rope-soled slippers offering silent yet sure footing. He moved swiftly but naturally, timing each movement to the stir of the wind, the rustle of the dry grass. Ki melted into the shadows as he stood looking, listening. It has been said of the practitioner of *ninjutsu* that "when looked for he cannot be seen." Ki had learned his lessons well, for even if one knew of his presence among the rocks he would not have been easily spotted.

In a surprisingly short time Ki returned, noiselessly dropping down at Jessie's side.

"It's just us and whoever's in that cabin," whispered Ki.

"There's only the one horse," Jessie answered.

Shrugging noncommittally, Ki replied, "That could be the trap."

"But I haven't seen any other prints, horse or boot," reasoned Jessie.

40

In an uncharacteristic gesture, Ki winked at her. "Good, Jessie, but never take anything for granted. Never fall prey to the unexpected."

Jessie smiled knowingly.

"I'll be careful," she said softly. But her jaw tightened. Down in that hut was a man who had shot at them. She wasn't going to forget that.

They started to move, Ki going to circle around back, Jessie moving slowly in on the front. But they instantly stopped in their tracks.

Coming down from the hills, three men on horseback approached the cabin. They were hard-looking men, all pressed from the same mold. They didn't have the toughness of the cowpuncher or the tenacity of the prospector. Even at this distance Jessie could see the ruthlessness in their eyes. They were hired killers.

Chapter 5

The riders stopped in front of the cabin. The lead man, distinguished by his pockmarked face made a quick gesture, and the third man, bringing up the rear, slid off his horse and scurried around to the side of the cabin. When he was in place, Pockmark nodded to his companion, then called out to the cabin in a deep, gravelly voice. From their place of concealment Jessie and Ki could clearly hear the words of the leader.

"McReedy! We're here to make a deal."

Jessie knew all about the types of deals these men made. She didn't need to see the henchman's hand resting lightly on his holstered .44 to smell a skunk. What she couldn't figure is why the skunks were having it out with each other. She turned to Ki, but all she saw was a fleeting shadow moving soundlessly among the rocks.

Pockmark was calling out once again, "We don't want no trouble, McReedy. C'mon out!"

The man beside the cabin had his rifle out and was

looking to the lead rider for some signal when the cabin door creaked open. A moment later a tall, lanky figure stepped into the doorway. Jessie leaned forward, trying to get a better look at the man half-hidden in the shadows of the dark cabin.

Pockmark lowered his voice, and Jessie had to strain to make out his words. "Step out into the light," he commanded, his tone calm yet threatening.

McReedy took a slow step out from the cabin.

"That's more like it," continued Pockmark. "Now hand over the ledger and we'll be on our way."

"I don't have it," McReedy answered in a not-so-steady voice. He looked around furtively and for a moment Jessie almost thought the man looked straight up at her. "But I can get it."

"He's lyin'," snapped the henchman.

"No," answered McReedy. "It's back along the trail, buried. . . ."

Pockmark cut him short. "I believe him, Jake." There was a snakelike venom to his words.

"I'll get my jacket and take you there." McReedy turned his back slowly and began to step back into the cabin. Perhaps because he was drawing on a man's back, Jake took the luxury of a slow draw. It was the last luxury of his life. Before his gun could be leveled, Jessie's shot rang out. She'd reacted instinctively; she just couldn't let a man be gunned down in cold blood—and in the back, no less! Her first shot caught Jake square in the chest, and the henchman dropped from his saddle. Immediately all hell broke loose.

McReedy quickly drew his gun and took a shot at Pockmark. But with Jessie's first shot the leader's horse had reared up, and McReedy hit the animal instead. The horse went down, spilling its rider. Pockmark rolled quickly out of the way but hesitated a moment, not knowing where the first shot had come from. Had McReedy stayed outside the cabin they would have had Pockmark trapped in a deadly crossfire, but instead McReedy chose to duck inside the safety of the cabin. Pockmark quickly scrambled to cover.

Jessie got off three quick shots before the third man pinned her down with his repeating Winchester. Jessie rolled to her right, then dodged to the next boulder. From there she moved down, unseen, closer to the cabin. Until she could get the rifleman, she would be unable to flush out Pockmark.

Resting against the boulder, Jessie took a moment to reload the four empty chambers of her six-shooter. She knew exactly where the rifleman was, but he couldn't be sure of her whereabouts. That gave her a slight advantage, and it was all she needed. She took a deep breath, readying herself. She stood up suddenly, exposed and open, but with a firm steady stance. The rifleman spotted her and turned, but it was too late. Jessie had already drawn a bead on the man. She fired two quick shots, then dropped down. One was all that was necessary. The rifleman fell against the cabin, then slumped to the ground.

Ki, meanwhile, had not been loafing. During the shooting he had been moving steadily toward Pockmark, and now was just one boulder above him. He stood up, ready to pounce, but as he did a shot rang out from the cabin. Alerted, Pockmark turned, gun drawn.

Ki's arm moved in a blur. The *shuriken* went whizzing through the air and sliced into Pockmark's arm. His gun dropped, unfired. With a yell Pockmark clawed at the round silver star.

He had barely pulled it out when Ki dropped down on him. Grabbing Pockmark by the lapels, Ki dropped to the ground and flipped the larger man through the air. Ki spun around and, as Pockmark staggered to his feet, let loose with a strong side-kick to the chest. Pockmark stumbled backwards, emerging from behind the cover of the rock. Suddenly there was a sharp crack from the cabin.

Pockmark fell, shot through the head. He was killed instantly.

Ki turned angrily. Had he wanted the man dead, the *shuriken* would have done the deed. He was using his knowledge of *jujitsu* to defeat Pockmark yet still keep him alive. There were questions to be answered. And now suddenly and senselessly it was over.

Ki turned to the cabin. A rifle jutted out from the window. But as Ki moved forward, the rifle was thrown to the ground. Slowly the door creaked open. Smiling, but with hands held high, McReedy stepped out of the cabin.

He hesitated briefly, but when he spotted Jessie, he lowered his arms and spoke.

"Evenin', Miss Starbuck."

Jessie, caught between anger and surprise, snapped quickly, "Three men and a horse lie dead, and all you've got to say is 'Evenin', Miss Starbuck'?"

McReedy smiled boyishly. "Sorry 'bout the horse."

Unable to stop herself, Jessie laughed freely. Truly, she herself felt more sympathy for the animal than for the plug-uglies. With that one remark McReedy had not only charmed Jessie but made it clear on which side of the fence he stood. Still, this was the man who had had Ki and her pinned down in a gully. One charming remark would not wipe the slate clean.

She studied McReedy silently. He stood about six feet and had a slight, wiry build that could probably move quickly and fluidly. Something in his pale blue eyes made her think of an antelope. He had a smooth curving jawline and a straight, narrow nose. There were no lines in his face, which had a soft, gentle look. And there was also his smile, very boyish and apologetic, as if he had just been caught with his hand in the cookie jar. Jessie, however, made a mental note not to underestimate him.

"I reckon you got a bit of explaining to do, Mister." Jessie said severely.

McReedy nodded and ushered them both inside the cabin.

Once inside, he walked to the far corner, bent down, and pried up a loose floorboard. He pulled out a large black ledger book and handed it to Jessie.

"This here is what all the fuss is about."

Jessie took it and leafed through the pages. It looked like any standard accounting book with records of payments made and received, land bought and sold.

McReedy continued, "When I first started to work for The Dobson Deed and Trust Company I figured they were like any big Eastern outfit coming out West to make their mark. And it seemed like a right smart thing for someone like me to get hooked up in. But it didn't take long to figure there was something crooked going on." He pointed to the book. "Towards the back there's a listing of deed transfers, and land purchases. All pretty regular if you don't know the lay of the land. But I used to do some surveying, and on a hunch I decided to look into one of those land purchases. Well, what I found didn't make no sense. It was a dry gulch! No one in his right mind would homestead land like that. And that's when I started getting real curious."

Jessie and Ki listened attentively. McReedy continued. "It seemed all the land transfers were being done at the central office in Waterville. I found that awfully odd. And I started checking the names. They seemed familiar, but they weren't from around these parts. No sir." He paused to swallow. "They were all on the board of trustees back East. I didn't know what to make of it at first. But it wasn't long before I saw some of the local homesteaders packin' up and pullin' out. Turned out they were workin' someone else's land. And we had the deeds to prove it. Well that's when I realized I was caught in a land swindle."

Jessie thought immediately of the Box H. "Is that what happened to Josh Hainley?"

McReedy nodded.

"A man like Hainley would have filed for his land," Jessie remarked.

"More than likely. But when the territorial deed office burned to the ground..."

"What about Washington?" Jessie asked.

McReedy shrugged. "What about it?"

"They should have the records—the Department of the Interior."

"First, we're just a territory out here. No one back in Washington gives a hoot. Who knows if they even keep deeds on file there? And secondly, when Eastern mucky-mucks have deeds to show proper ownership of the land, it don't matter much what some sodbuster or cowpuncher can show."

"But the Box H was an established outfit," Jessie protested to no one in particular.

McReedy didn't disagree. "Josh Hainley was smart enough to realize he was getting pulled into a fight he couldn't win."

"But the land was rightfully his," Jessie countered.

"The Dobson Company no doubt has a passel of lawyers to prove the contrary."

"Well, we can have lawyers of our own," Jessie said firmly.

47

"You also have some hard proof that something phony has been going on." McReedy pointed to the ledger.

"That's why your friends outside wanted it," Jessie asked.

"Yeh." McReedy nodded. "But they're no friends of mine. They do Dobson's dirty work. When a man don't know he's been beat, those hombres help him see the light."

Jessie understood what that meant. "They came to a just end," she said to herself. Then she turned to McReedy with another question. "Where did we fit in?"

"You mean why was I taking shots at you the other day?"

Jessie nodded.

"Actually, it was a simple mistake."

"People who shoot at me usually find out it was a big mistake," she said seriously.

"You see, before I realized what I was dealing with, I asked a few rather impertinent questions. Or maybe I should say I asked the wrong folks the wrong questions. Of course once I realized I was in the middle of some kind of swindle it was too late. I had already shown my hand."

"I see," Jessie muttered. She was recalling Ki's early hypothesis, and had the feeling that Ki was once again right. McReedy's next words proved it.

"I've been expecting Jake and his sidekicks to pay me a visit for some time now. When I saw you two coming out to the cabin I didn't want to take any chances."

"But how could you mistake us for them?" Jessie wondered aloud.

McReedy shifted uneasily. "Well, I saw your friend leading the way, and to be honest, ma'am"—he fidgeted nervously—"I just didn't realize you was a female."

Jessie laughed, partially at his discomfort, and partially

because it was not the first time that mistake had been made. Jessie did many things like a man; ride, rope, shoot. It did not embarrass her; she took it as a compliment. After all, she had no insecurities about her femininity. When it mattered most, she would never, ever be mistaken for a man.

There were still some things that needed explaining. "But once I called out to you?" Jessie asked.

"By then I began thinking I had made a mistake. That's when I started aiming for the dirt."

"Why did you keep shooting at all?"

"A good question," McReedy conceded. "I don't know if I have a good answer. All's I can say is I needed some time to think it through."

Jessie wasn't thrilled with the answer, but she understood and accepted it. When under fire, men could not always be expected to think rationally. Especially those men who did not as a regular course find themselves in that situation. Looking at McReedy she doubted if anyone had ever tried to shoot him or gun him down before. He couldn't be expected to keep a calm head.

McReedy continued, "The only thing I could think of was to keep you pinned till nightfall, then hightail it out of there. Somewhere along the way I figured maybe this was the best thing that could have happened."

"How so?" Jessie asked.

"Well, I knew there was no place to run, and I realized it might be good to have someone like you on my side."

"You expected we'd show up like the cavalry and—" Jessie began.

"Not exactly. I was hopin' you'd show up before them" —he jerked his thumb to the door—"so I could hand you that ledger. I didn't rightly know what I should do with it. And I knew something of your reputation, Miss Starbuck."

49

"Then it's pretty lucky we showed up when we did," Jessie said warmly.

McReedy looked away. "I reckon so, but I don't feel lucky. I feel pretty low."

There was a moment of silence. Then Ki stood up. "I better go and get our horses, Jessie, before it gets too dark."

McReedy stood up too. "I'll give you a hand."

Ki shook his head. "I'll make better time alone."

Ki left, and McReedy sat back down. But he seemed ill at ease, and after a moment, he stepped outside. Jessie continued to study the ledger, but soon after stepped outside too.

"What I can't figure—" she started to ask but suddenly stopped. McReedy was sitting on the floor, his back resting against the cabin. In the fading light his face seemed younger and softer. His skin was smooth and his pale blue eyes had an almost childish innocence to them. But around the edges Jessie perceived a deep sorrow. She dropped down next to him. McReedy did not turn to her, but spoke softly, almost as if he were speaking to himself.

"The worse part is I helped cheat all them honest folks. I'm no better than the worst of 'em."

"No, you didn't realize—"

"I'm a swindler and a cheat, no different from the rest of 'em."

Suddenly Jessie felt very compassionate. There were cheats and scoundrels and land swindles in every new territory. There were men who thought it easiest to prey on others, men who got rich lying, cheating, and murdering. Men who deserved nothing more than a well-placed bullet or a rope around their necks. But McReedy was not one of them.

McReedy was an honest man caught in a whirl of deceptions. Here was another victim. He didn't lose his land or his money, but he was a victim just the same. She leaned forward and kissed him lightly on the cheek. He looked at her, puzzled.

"I know you're different," she said at last, in a soft, comforting voice. She leaned forward again, resting her head on his shoulder.

"Sometimes we get rustled up in things we never reckoned with," she said heavily. Her voice was thick with weariness of the seemingly endless fight against injustice.

He slipped his hand behind her neck and gently caressed her. "How can you know so much?" he said in a whisper.

Jessie lifted her head and looked into his eyes. Suddenly she recalled all the good men who had spent their lives fighting against corruption, greed, and downright meanness. And she remembered all the men who died in that fight, including her father, Alex. The emotion came welling up inside her.

She found her lips pressing against his. It was a soft, lingering kiss, full of tenderness, and when Jessie pulled back, McReedy looked apologetic.

"I'm sorry, Miss Starbuck."

Jessie laughed teasingly. "If you kiss me again, you'll have to call me Jessie." And with that she pressed her lips against his, this time not holding back. Her tongue sought out his, playing with it, teasing it, swallowing it.

McReedy pulled away. "We shouldn't be doing this. What about Ki?"

Jessie looked disappointed. A warm glow was just beginning to spread over her. Her strawberry nipples were proudly erect, and pressing lightly against her shirt. "We have plenty of time," she said.

McReedy looked offended. "I may have swindled hon-

51

est people by mistake, but I ain't about to steal another man's woman."

Jessie took hold of his hand and held it up to her lips. "Ki is the oldest and most trusted friend I have." She sucked his finger seductively. "He's like a brother to me." She let go of his fingers and they dropped to her firm, rounded breasts.

"Well then, call me Chase." McReedy's fingers began to roam around Jessie's breasts, teasing her hard, erect nipples. Jessie straddled him.

Kneeling over him, it wasn't long before he had her flannel shirt unbuttoned and had replaced his fingers with his hungry mouth. Jessie moaned softly and quickly opened Chase's shirt, tracing his smooth but muscular chest with her fingers. McReedy put his arm around her and pulled her close to him, sucking hard on her breasts.

Jessie leaned back and reached for his crotch. Even through his heavy britches she could feel his manhood throbbing. She deftly undid his buttons and managed to pull out his growing erection. She began stroking it lightly, but soon felt that hot, burning sensation in her loins. She pulled her breast away from Chase's mouth and let go of his rigid member.

"Don't . . ." he said huskily.

Jessie said nothing, but began to shimmy out of her tight jeans. Her long, muscular legs and the soft curves of her hips reflected like white alabaster in the pale moonlight. She removed her shirt, exposing her ripe breasts to the night air. Chase sighed appreciatively. His eyes followed the curves of her body down her flat stomach, to focus on a small tuft of downy soft hair.

As she moved over him, he could smell the warm muskiness of her arousal. Her silken mound brushed his face. He reached around her, pulling her to him, burying his face

52

into her womanness. Jessie moaned and leaned forward, resting against the wall of the cabin for support. She ran her fingers through Chase's light brown hair as he moved his head in slow, sensual circles. Jessie let out a soft "ooh" as she slowly became engulfed in a sea of pleasure. She floated weightlessly, her whole being centered in the soft folds of her mound.

McReedy's tongue, light and flicking at first, now became deep and probing. Her knees began to tremble, and Chase pressed her closer to him. As he held her tight she felt the first wave break. It began somewhere deep in her loins, and with a sudden shudder and a gasp Jessie collapsed against Chase's strong torso. She gasped again, this time with surprise and delight, as she felt his hard, tumescent shaft enter her slowly. She arched her back and squeezed his manhood tight.

This time it was Chase who gasped. Jessie slowly and rhythmically rolled her pelvis, riding his erection like a weathervane in the breeze. Chase lay there quietly, but then began slow, deliberate thrusts deep inside her. They moved now in unison, slowly and passionately. Chase reached up and grabbed Jessie's breasts, massaging them, caressing them, sucking on her nipples. Jessie began to grip him tightly, rippling his shaft with her inner muscles. She smiled as Chase began to groan loudly. His thrusts came quicker. She matched his every move, and as her swollen breasts bobbed against Chase's darting tongue, a soft, red blush began spreading across her body. She began to feel the tension mount, her floodgates about to open. She reached behind her, grabbed his sack in her palm, and rubbed it softly.

"No, not yet," he said hoarsely. Jessie ignored him and continued to rub his scrotum with a soft, steady pressure, and soon he was pleading with her: "Oh, don't stop."

Chase furiously pounded his iron-hard tool into her. As she felt her orgasm begin she squeezed him tightly. He exploded suddenly, his load shooting deep inside her.

His powerful contractions sent her over the edge, and they climaxed together. Each of her spasms milked his shaft, each spurting of his sending ripples of pleasure through her. After what seemed like an eternity, Jessie lowered her head, her hair brushing against Chase's bare chest. He pulled her to him and kissed her passionately. She began to feel him harden inside her once again, and much against her desires, drew off of him.

"I'm sorry, but we better get inside now."

It was Chase's turn to smile. "There's nothing to be sorry for."

"Oh there is. I'm sorry we can't stay out here and make love all night long."

★

Chapter 6

When Ki returned he found Jessie asleep on one of the two cots. McReedy, stretched out on the floor, had saved the other cot for Ki. It was a thoughtful gesture, though Ki would have been just as happy on the floor. But it seemed pointless to wake McReedy simply to offer him the cot, so Ki took it for himself.

He didn't fall asleep right away. They had caught up with McReedy, and had found out what had happened to Josh Hainley and his Box H, but things were far from settled. In fact they had become much more complicated. Jessie's aim had not been merely to track down McReedy; it was to find the ones responsible for the swindle. If McReedy had been guilty, if he had been the one who was cheating men out of their lands, the matter would be over. But he was not the mastermind; he was only a cog in the works. To get to the bottom of things would require a lot more. There were too many unknowns, too many missing pieces for Ki to formulate a plan. He did not doubt that the ledger in McReedy's possesion could supply many of the answers, but would it supply the proof they needed to see the wrongs righted and the guilty parties brought to justice? Ki couldn't say. He turned over and went to sleep.

Morning was celebrated with a stack of flapjacks and a pot of hot coffee. Today no one was on the run, no one was hot on the trail. There was no need to worry about the smoke from their fire giving away their position. And most importantly, there was no need to get in the saddle at the crack of dawn.

Jessie let business go until after her second cup of coffee, when she turned to Ki. "After breakfast I'd like you to take a close look at that ledger."

Ki nodded. "I've already given it a lot of thought, Jessie. I think it'll give us the names of the guilty people. But proving that they are indeed guilty will be something entirely different."

McReedy agreed. "They've got enough legal papers to back up anything they've done. It'll be hard to catch 'em."

"That's if we follow the letter of the law, Mr. McReedy," Jessie said sternly. "There's more than one way to smoke a weasel from its hole."

"What are you suggesting, Jessie?" he asked excitedly.

"Right now, I don't know. But when the time comes we'll know what to do." She shot Ki a sly grin. "By the time we get to Waterville, Ki will have thought of something."

Ki couldn't help but smile back. "Why Waterville?" he asked.

She turned to McReedy. "Isn't that where you said the central office was?"

McReedy nodded. "The central office for the Northwest division," he clarified.

56

"What do you expect to find there that isn't in the ledger we already have?" Ki asked.

"It's not what, it's who," Jessie answered. "What we need to do is get our hooks into someone who knows what's going on."

Ki didn't disagree, but he saw it slightly differently. "Why not go straight to the top?" he asked. He turned to McReedy. "Is there a Mr. Dobson?"

"There sure is," he replied enthusiastically. "Right smack in the middle of Waterville."

"Waterville?" Jessie sounded confused. "I thought you said it was an Eastern outfit?"

"It is. Out of Baltimore. Phineas Dobson founded the firm. Delbert Dobson, his grandson, is in charge of the whole Western region. And like I said, he makes his home in Waterville."

"Is he the head of the company?" Ki asked.

"That I can't say for sure, but I doubt it. He has two brothers, both older. I reckon they carry the majority of the stock. At best he's a junior partner. But I can't be certain that's a fact."

Jessie thought it over. "It sounds right. There would be too many ties and business associates back East for the head of the company to pick up and relocate out here." Her eyes narrowed as she looked at McReedy. "From what you know, Chase, could any of this be going on without Delbert Dobson's knowledge?"

"To be honest, I can't rightly say. That someone up high is calling the shots I'm sure of. But it might be someone in the Baltimore office."

"Someone here has to know what's going on," Ki said.

McReedy nodded. "True, but that someone doesn't have to be Delbert."

57

"We'll find out soon enough," Jessie said firmly. "No use flapping about it now."

That was the end of the discussion.

Ki and McReedy went out and buried the three plug-uglies, but not before Ki had searched them. He found nothing of any interest.

It was an easy four-day ride to Waterville. There was no rush, no reason to push it. Jessie didn't expect the situation to change in the next few days. Dobson, or whoever the mastermind of the swindle was, had no reason to think anyone was onto him. That is, anyone save for McReedy. And men had been sent out to deal with him.

McReedy seemed a little nervous about that. One night he mentioned it to Jessie. "When Jake and his pals don't show, someone's going to get wise," he began.

"I wouldn't worry about that much, Chase."

"I'm the worryin' kind," he said without a smile.

"They couldn't make it back to Waterville any sooner than us," she said simply.

He nodded but didn't seem satisfied. "What if they were supposed to send a wire?"

Jessie smiled. "You are the worrying kind."

"Can't help it," he said with a grin. "My daddy used to tell me there were two kinds of folks, those with fast guns and the rest of us which worry 'bout it." He gave a small chuckle. "And I ain't the fastest draw around."

"And my father used to say that guns don't solve everything," Jessie remarked.

"But he was handy with a gun, wasn't he?"

Jessie nodded. "He taught me everything I know."

"Does that include staying calm and not fretting?"

Again she nodded. "But Ki also had a hand in that."

"He ain't a bad shot himself," McReedy added.

Ki then spoke up. "As I recall you did a fair piece of shooting when you dropped that plug-ugly with one shot."

"A rifle's one thing, Ki. I ain't half bad with one. But a six-shooter's something else again."

"In the end they both get the job done," Ki noted dryly.

"I reckon so. But I was brought up thinking there was a difference. A rifle's for hunting; a revolver's for killing."

Jessie had a hunch about what was bothering McReedy. "Killing in cold blood is one thing, Chase. Killing in self-defense, or in the defense of others, is something else entirely."

"I reckon so."

For a while, that seemed the end of the discussion. But a few minutes later, McReedy started it again. "I'm still a mite concerned, Jessie," he began. "Eventually, Dobson will realize that his plug-uglies ain't returning. . . ."

"There'll be a whole lot of days that'll pass before he realizes it."

"You seem awfully sure of it."

"Of course. First of all, if you had headed east instead of west, it'd take that many more days for them to have caught up with you. They were coming from the west, weren't they?" McReedy nodded. Jessie continued, "And if you had fled instead of fighting it would have been another couple of days till they caught up to you a second time."

"But what if they telegraphed?"

Jessie smiled. "Chase, you think like a businessman, not a swindler. I doubt an upstanding, respectable citizen like Dobson wants to have it known he associates with the likes of those who came after you. A telegram would raise some embarrassing questions for our friend Dobson."

McReedy didn't look convinced. "I have Will Grant send me wires any time he runs into a problem."

Jessie had to laugh. "Hired guns aren't errand boys, Chase. Those types don't answer to anyone till it's time to pick up the rest of their bounty."

"Oh."

"You don't have anything to worry about," Ki said kindly. "Jessie has experience with these types. She knows exactly how to handle them."

"I reckon so," McReedy muttered. "I've heard some about the Starbuck empire. The cattle ranches, the mining companies, the timber mills, the holdings in railroads . . ."

"We're somewhat familiar with them, too," Ki said with a smile.

McReedy looked embarrassed. "But I never realized that it involved, well, dealings with . . ." He seemed lost for the right words. "I think what I'm trying to say is I always pictured it being run from the confines of a paneled office."

Ki laughed. "Maybe that's the way other people would run the business, but not Jessie."

"There's a lot that has to be done, Chase—a lot that has to be set straight. And I can't trust anyone to do it but Ki and myself."

"You must do all right at it," McReedy observed.

We're still alive, she thought to herself. But she didn't say it. Instead she looked McReedy square in the eye. "We do all right," she agreed.

Ki smiled at Jessie's modest understatement. He considered remaining silent, but changed his mind. His comment was directed to Jessie as well as McReedy. "We do a damn sight better than just all right." His grin only partially masked the seriousness of his words.

* * *

A half-day out of Waterville they made camp. The spot they chose was situated about a mile from the road to town, and it was unlikely they would be discovered. Even if someone wandered off the trail, the box elders and bullberries offered concealment from the casual observer. There was also good grazing and a small stream sheltered by a grove of willows.

Delbert Dobson had only met McReedy once, but that was one time more than Jessie would have liked. The last thing they needed was to have McReedy identified, not only because it would make things tough for McReedy, possibly endangering his life, but because it would also shackle Jessie and Ki. As of yet they didn't have an exact plan, but Ki was going to go into town and feel around. If he were to be associated with McReedy it would seriously hamper his ability to gather information.

McReedy understood why he shouldn't risk going into town, and though it was a comfortable camp, he suggested that Jessie and Ki stay in town at the hotel. They both refused. Until they knew the role Jessie would play, the pose she would adopt, it was best for Ki to go in alone. If anyone could gather information and fit the pieces together it was Ki.

They had all agreed they couldn't simply march right in and accuse Dobson to his face. Besides the fact that he would be able to deny the charges, there was a good possibility that Dobson would have them all thrown into jail as crooks, scoundrels, cheats, or slanderers. For similiar reasons Jessie didn't think going to the sheriff was a good idea either. There was no doubt Dobson was the big cheese in Waterville. He would call all the shots. Even if the sheriff was essentially honest, Dobson would have a lot of say.

And chances were good the sheriff was less then totally honest.

In fact, Jessie had her suspicions about Dobson and Waterville. She discussed them with Ki as he saddled up. "I'd be very careful in town," she began.

Ki's polite smile told her she was stating the obvious. "I'm always careful, Jessie." It was not so much a boast as simple truth.

"I know," Jessie replied. "But you won't know who you'll be talking to."

Again Ki nodded.

Jessie continued. "I wouldn't trust anybody," she warned.

Ki was patient. "I usually don't."

"I know," she said again.

"Is there something else bothering you, Jessie?"

"Yes," she said with a nod. "But I can't quite put my finger on it."

"Well, don't worry. I've gone into unfriendly, hostile towns before."

"That's it, Ki. I realize what's wrong."

"All right, let's hear it."

"Did you ever wonder why someone like Dobson would settle in Waterville?"

"I don't find it odd just because he's an Easterner and he's rich, if that's what you're getting at. Maybe he likes green grass and open skies."

"I find it odd that he didn't set up shop in Helena," Jessie answered.

Ki thought it over. "The territorial capital would be an obvious choice," he agreed.

"Except for a few things. Like a U.S. marshal."

"Ah-ha," Ki said with a nod.

"And a few million dollars in gold ore."

"You lost me there, Jessie."

"Helena, besides having a marshal, is a rich town, Ki. A lot of gold and silver comes out of there. That means not only are there rich miners and mining companies, there are rich bankers, freight companies, probably a lot of Eastern syndicates as well."

"I see. And Waterville has none of that."

Jessie smiled. "Exactly."

"So you think Dobson would be just another powerful businessman in a town like Helena. Whereas he's the number one honcho in a place like Waterville."

"A big fish in a small pond," Jessie said.

"I'll be careful, Jessie," he said as he swung up into the saddle.

"Remember, Ki, I suspect he practically owns the town."

Ki waved farewell then started his horse towards the trail. Jessie watched him ride away.

Chapter 7

Waterville was a small, dismal town. It was basically one street long, with houses, cabins, and shacks randomly spread out around it. There was no pattern to the layout. At least, no pattern that Ki could discern.

While the major street did have a restaurant, hotel, bank, telegraph office, and other various merchants, there were also a few abandoned buildings, a clear sign that many people had packed up shop and moved elsewhere.

Jessie's interest in why a wealthy man like Dobson should settle in a town like Waterville was well founded. There were no amenities suited to a man of riches, and as far as Ki could see, no reason why a man who could pick and choose his abode would choose Waterville. Ki had seen much worse, but there would have been no problem finding a nicer town. There must be a good reason why Dobson came here, and Ki was going to find out what it was.

It turned dark as Ki put his horse up in livery, and that

suited him fine. The best place to find out about any town was always the saloon. And though saloons would always have a few customers regardless of the time of day, the evenings were when things picked up. That would give Ki the widest chance to find what he was looking for, while —and this was equally important—raising the fewest number of questions about himself. A barkeep who had nothing to do but wipe the bar and pour an occasional drink would often eye a passing stranger with curious interest. But at this time of day any saloon worth its shingle should have the barman too busy to make idle conversation.

The Mad Dog Saloon was a modest drinking establishment, and very little else. Throughout the West, where "saloon" could also mean gambling room, dance hall, restaurant, and brothel, it surprised Ki to see nothing but a bar and a few small tables. The Mad Dog's specialty was drinking, and nothing but.

But none of the clientele seemed to mind that the saloon had limited fare. A row of men lined the bar, and some of the tables were occupied. Ki studied the assemblage; there was nothing remarkable or unusual about the men. He moved to the bar and ordered a beer, but before it came he heard someone wisecrack in a deep voice, "Damned if the coolies ain't landed."

Ki ignored the remark. His beer came and he placed his money on the bar.

The wisecracker moved closer. "Don't they got whiskey where you come from?"

Ki turned to face the questioner. He was a husky man with broad shoulders, a thick neck, and meaty fists. His hat, far back on his head, showed a rounded forehead and greasy brown hair. From the slur of his words and the look in his eyes, the man appeared to be slightly drunk.

Ki turned away without answering. He wasn't afraid of

the man; he just didn't want to cause trouble and draw attention to himself. But the wisecracker wasn't to be so easily dismissed.

"You just off the boat, boy?" the man snapped. "'Cause in this country, when a man asks a question, it's polite to answer."

"Hey, Colligan, maybe he don't speak any English," his friend shouted out.

"Don't be an idiot, Brunner. He ordered beer, didn't he?"

"Reckon so," his friend answered.

The wisecracker turned back to Ki. "Of course, maybe you don't care about being polite and friendly-like. Otherwise a man answers when spoken to."

It was a direct challenge that Ki couldn't ignore. "I come from San Francisco," he said simply.

"Don't they drink whiskey there?" Colligan demanded.

"They do. I don't."

"Well you do now." Colligan turned to the bartender. "A bottle and another glass."

Colligan was looking for trouble, but he wasn't necessarily looking for a fight. If he had wanted a fight he would have said a few derogatory remarks to Ki. The color of his skin, or the smell of an Oriental, was a common enough place to begin. He then would have demanded that Ki leave the saloon. Whether Ki left of his own free will or whether he was booted out wouldn't matter. Either way, men like Colligan had their fun.

That Colligan wanted his fun at the expense of Ki was evident. But that fun didn't have to lead to a fight. Colligan looked like he won more than his fair share of fist-fights. In fact, he had probably won so many fights, the actual ass-kicking gave him only minor satisfaction. Ki suspected the threat of violence was only an inducement to get others to do his bidding, rather than being an end in itself.

"Whoo-ee, another drunk Chinee," Brunner yelled happily.

"We'll see," Colligan said with a smile.

"Don't count yer chickens yet, boys," the bartender said as he placed a bottle of whiskey in front of Colligan. He turned to Ki. "Nobody in the Mad Dog drinks unless he wants to."

"That's a new one to me," Colligan said with surprise.

"That's the way it is. You drink what you want. But if yer friend wants to pass . . ."

"It ain't like you to side with a coolie," Colligan said unhappily.

"Yeh, we just want to have a little fun," Brunner added.

"Have yer fun out back in the alley. You and your Chinaman can drink all you want out there."

"I ain't no saddle tramp that's going to drink out in an alley," Colligan protested. His mood was turning nasty. "Besides, I ain't forcing no one to have a drink." He turned to Ki. "You are going to have a drink with me, ain't you friend?"

"I'll have one," Ki said coldly. Colligan beamed.

The bartender slammed a shotglass down in front of Ki, but eyed Colligan threateningly. "I'm warning you, Colligan, this Chinaman gets sick and makes a mess all over my bar and you're going to clean it up."

"Keep yer hat on," Colligan growled. He filled Ki's glass and refilled his own. "Drink up, boy," he said with a mean smile.

Ki tossed back his drink.

"You look like you could use another," Colligan said as he refilled Ki's glass.

The bartender looked uneasy. "Why bother, Colligan?"

67

"They ain't as much fun as Injuns," he answered. "But they'll do in a pinch."

The bartender shook his head. "He's probably a relative of Chen's . . ."

"Chen? Dobson's houseboy?" Brunner interrupted.

The bartender nodded and looked to Colligan. "Give him a break."

Colligan smiled. "He can stop any time he wants," he said simply. But his tone implied just the opposite. Ki realized he might have been wrong. Maybe Colligan was looking for a fight. Ki was tempted to give the man exactly what he was looking for. No doubt there would be a surprise or two. But teaching Colligan a lesson might cost Ki more than it was worth. The recognition that would come from beating up the bully would make Ki a well-known figure in town. That would make it difficult to carry on a discreet investigation of Dobson. Therefore, Ki vowed to refrain from kicking Colligan's ass, at least for the time being.

Ki picked up the glass and downed its contents.

As soon as the glass hit the bar, Colligan filled it a third time. "Our Chinee is a real drinker, ain't he fellas? Help yerself," he said to Ki. "But from here on out the drinks are on you." He poured himself a shot, then turned to his friend. "Brunner?" The man nodded and Colligan filled his friend's glass also. Then he looked Ki cold in the eye. "You don't want me to drink alone, now do you?" His hand swept across the saloon. "These here are my friends. If I drink they drink."

Ki returned the stare. "Why don't you just stick your hand in my pocket and take all my money? It would be faster, and more honest. Or are you the type that prefers to bushwack a man from a dry gulch?"

68

Colligan's face reddened. "I'm going to pretend I didn't hear that," he hissed.

Ki was tiring of the game. Besides, he'd already heard something that gave him an idea. Unfortunately, he couldn't act too tough or his plan wouldn't work.

He picked up his drink and flung it into Colligan's face. There was a moment of silence as the liquor dripped down the man's face.

Colligan wiped his eyes with the back of his hand, then formed his fingers into a fist and swung out at Ki.

Ki could see it coming, but made no move to avoid the blow. It hit him square in the jaw but had little impact. There was a lot of muscle behind it, but Ki timed it perfectly, and rolled his head with the impact.

As he snapped his head back he staggered backwards, and after two steps crashed into a table and went down.

He wondered if his little charade would fool anyone. But as it turned out there wasn't a soul in the saloon who didn't believe Colligan had knocked the Chinee out with one punch. Apparently he had accomplished similar feats in the past, and his knockout punch was well-known.

Colligan was quick to boast about his punch, and if there was a witness present who doubted the truth, he kept it to himself. Ki lay on the floor with his eyes closed. He felt hands picking him up. Someone else grabbed his legs.

"Let's get him over to the stable," he heard someone say.

Ki thought about opening his eyes, but then he heard someone else remark, "He's out cold," and Ki decided not to disappoint them. He kept his eyes shut till he felt himself being dropped into a stall of dry hay.

There was no reason to get up; there was nothing that

had to be done. Ki lay there, with his eyes closed, and was soon fast asleep.

He didn't get up till morning.

Sunlight brought a slightly different perspective to Waterville. The town hadn't improved any, but the scenery had. Waterville was tucked right at the edge of timber country, on the shores of what was a tributary of the Missouri River. It was situated at the spot where deep, rolling forests turned into rocky meadow.

That explained something of its history and design. Ki guessed that Waterville was first a trapping outpost. Trappers would ship their pelts down the river and spend their money in town. As more and more trappers came into the area, more cabins were built, and Waterville grew. That would in part explain the lack of urban planning and the willy-nilly outbreak of houses every which way. Trappers built their storage shacks or one-room cabins anywhere they pleased, not realizing that a town, not just an outpost, would soon be the result.

At one time Waterville seemed to be looking at prosperity. Then the rosy future had come to an abrupt end, when gold was discovered further north. The trapping industry was soon played out, and Waterville's status dropped to second-rate. The town was still in a picturesque setting and the surrounding land was just as beautiful, but scenery doesn't feed a hungry mouth. Folks moved on to greener pastures. Ki did not doubt that Delbert Dobson was responsible in one way or another for a large part of the jobs in town.

After looking for and not finding the stablehand, Ki walked over to the general store.

He walked in and asked the proprietor where he might find Mr. Dobson.

The storekeeper eyed him carefully. "You're the fella that got knocked out last night, ain't ya?"

Ki didn't bother answering, and the storekeeper continued, "Well, you don't look any worse for the wear. Care for a cup of coffee? I got a hot pot on."

Ki accepted the offer.

The storekeeper returned and handed him a steaming cup. "You must be looking for Chen."

Ki had decided last night that the person he had to get to know was this Chen. He nodded.

"He was in early this morning to drop off an order. He should be back by three."

Ki thanked him for the coffee and the information and left.

He walked over to the restaurant and ordered a plate of flapjacks and ham. The middle-aged woman who ran the establishment watched Ki devour his breakfast, and when the plate was cleared, she returned with a second stack. He took his time on these, and in between bites he asked a few subtle questions. What information he found out about Dobson, McReedy had already told him. Ki wanted an idea of how these people felt toward the wealthy Easterner, but he couldn't quite come right out and ask.

He finished his second portion of flapjacks and wiped his mouth with the muslin napkin.

"For a skinny fellow, you sure can pack it away," the woman said. "Like another?"

Ki shook his head. "But it was awfully good, ma'am. If I could afford it, I'd eat here every day."

"Why, thank you," she said as she blushed.

71

"A man like Mr. Dobson must be in here every day," he said casually.

The woman laughed. "Why, I hardly ever see Mr. Dobson."

"That so? Can't figure why anyone would pass up all this."

"He got his own cook. But he sends over here for pies and such. No one makes a cobbler like I do," she said proudly. "Care for a piece? Berry, made just last night, an' almost still warm."

"Sold. From the minute you said berry," Ki said with a smile. "It's my favorite."

"You and Dobson. There's another one just baked for him."

"Chen picking it up later?"

The woman nodded, showing no surprise over his question.

A moment later she placed the pie down in front of him.

"How long has Chen been doing that?" he asked as he picked up his fork.

"I don't follow . . ." she began at first. Then she seemed to catch on. "You mean coming by here for pies?"

Ki nodded as he took his first bite.

"Since he first came to work for Dobson . . ."

Ki nodded, trying to encourage her to finish the thought.

"I reckon that must be going on now a little bit more'n a year," she added.

Ki swallowed and smiled.

"You look very pleased," the woman said proudly.

Ki nodded. "I do believe I'll have to have another piece, ma'am."

The pie was indeed excellent. But the information was even better.

The people of Waterville seemed fairly friendly. Ki decided not to judge the town by its looks or the handful of men he had encountered at the bar.

Ki would have liked to have had a look around the outskirts of town, possibly even ride out to the Dobson house, which was only a few miles upriver, but he dared not leave for fear of missing Chen.

He went to the hotel, a run-down, fleabag establishment, and judged it not much better than his accommodations at the stable. Ki would not have played it this way originally, but now it suited his purpose to be a penniless, down-on-his-luck drifter. It was not uncommon for drifters and cowhands to bed down with their horses. Ki certainly didn't mind. He would continue to hang his hat in the stall at the livery.

He went back there and spent the rest of the morning listening to the livery owner talk about the good old days in Waterville. Ki's assessment of the town had been correct. But interestingly enough, the man's outlook for the future was optimistic.

"Yep, this town ain't seen the last of the good times."

"That so?"

The man nodded. "And I ain't the only one that thinks so."

"You mean Dobson?" Ki asked outright.

"It don't hurt having a monied dude, but with or without, the times'll change."

"Dobson must have helped through the slow times."

"True enough," the liveryman agreed. "He just about kept the bank open singlehandedly. Without his dealin's we'd have to ride more'n forty miles for the nearest bank. An' without him there ain't enough money in town to keep

73

even a wall safe near-filled. An' half the sundries that come through here are for him an' his house guests."

"He keep a lot of company?" Ki asked.

"There's always a fair amount of folks payin' a visit. Business associates an' relatives, I reckon." He paused a moment to recollect, then broke into a hearty laugh. "A lot of green dudes, I'll say that much," he said as he shook his head.

"You'd think after all this time the green would harden some," Ki remarked. "This country would harden most . . ."

"Or kill them right quick," the man added.

"True enough," agreed Ki. "And Dobson hasn't been buried yet."

The man smiled. "He ain't been toughened up all that much either."

"Once a dude, always a dude." Ki continued to try and pry whatever he could from the man.

"More'n likely. But truth be told, I don't get to see him all that much. Like I said, he's done a lot to hold this town together."

Ki realized the man had nothing more to tell him about Dobson. But he still wanted to know about the town's future. "Till the good times roll in again?" he began.

The livery man nodded.

"Any idea when?" Ki prodded.

"Not long, I reckon. Now that the Northern Pacific is up an' running, it's only a matter of time till they run a spur line down to Helena."

"Seems likely enough."

"It's more'n likely, friend, it's a fact. And when they do, they'll run it straight down through here."

Ki looked skeptical, but only to draw the man out more. The livery man smiled and continued, "This ain't just my

74

scuttlebutt. It's clear enough to me that Dobson is betting on it, too."

"Really, now?"

The man nodded. "Why else would he be buyin' up all the land he can get his hands on?"

Why indeed, Ki thought to himself.

"Payin' top dollar, too," the man added. "Rich folk don't get that way for spendin' money foolishly. No sir, if he's buyin', the railroad's comin'."

"And when it does?" Ki asked, playing dumb.

"It'll open up this whole territory. An' we won't just be a whistle-stop town either. No sir-ree."

Ki knew that was so. He also knew that Dobson's business transactions, or at least those of the Dobson Deed and Trust Company, were less than honest. He wondered what was really at stake.

"What the river once did for this town, the railroad will do again," concluded the liveryman. "You just wait and see."

Ki said he might just do that, and moved on.

The next stop was the sheriff. Ki had a good guess what he'd find, but he wanted to be sure. He walked to the jail, a solid, baked-brick construction, and opened a thick pine door.

A tall, lanky man with wavy, black hair and a thick mustache looked out from underneath his Stetson. "Can I help you?" he asked, not removing his feet from the desk.

"You the sheriff?" Ki asked.

The man spread his arms. "Ain't no one else here."

"I'd like to report an attack," Ki said.

There was interest and excitement in his voice as the sheriff swung down his legs. "Indians? There ain't been Indian troubles for, oh . . ."

"Not Indians," Ki clarified. "White men. Right here in town. Over at the saloon."

"The Mad Dog?" the sheriff asked.

Ki mimicked the man's gesture. "Is there another one?"

The sheriff was not amused. "I didn't hear of no complaints . . ." he began.

"I'm filing one now."

"All right, what happened?"

Ki began to tell him about the fight with Colligan.

"Were there any witnesses besides this fellow Colligan?"

"There was a saloon full of people," Ki answered.

"Any names? Do you have any of their names?"

Ki shook his head.

"Well, I'll look into it," promised the sheriff. "But without any witnesses, it's just your word against his."

"As I recall, there was more than one man in there laughing it up. I'm sure you'll be able to find one man who remained sober enough to remember what happened."

The sheriff picked at his teeth. "Don't know. If no one comes forward . . . Look, friend, seems like no harm was done. My advice is get on yer horse and keep ridin'. And consider yourself lucky."

Ki had heard enough. There was no justice to be had here. But it wasn't justice he was looking for when he had entered the office. He wanted to know what kind of man the sheriff was. He had his answer.

It would be no surprise to find out that the Dobson Deed and Trust Company paid the man's salary.

As he walked down the street, Ki's mind was on the sheriff, and he realized just how accurate Jessie's hunch was. Because of the fact that he was deep in thought, he didn't notice it at first.

The man coming out of the restaurant looked like any other man. It could be anyone carrying a pie in each hand. It wasn't until the man had climbed into the wagon that Ki put two and two together.

He broke into a run.

With a snap of the reins the two quarter-horses surged forward. It didn't take them long to get the wagon up to speed.

As the buckboard turned the corner, Ki was certain he saw the driver's Oriental profile. There was no mistaking the slanting eyes of what had to be Chen.

Chapter 8

For a moment, Jessie experienced a bit of concern as she watched Ki ride off. But she quickly talked herself out of it. She knew there was little reason to worry. Ki could take care of himself. He had proved that many times over. Jessie couldn't think of a better person to have at her side than Ki. No matter what the fight, or what the odds, with Ki alongside, there was a good chance of winning. She knew that, yet she still worried about him.

She laughed as she walked back to the camp. There were times when the boot was on the other foot, when she had gone off and left Ki behind. And regardless of what she had said to him, he still worried. She realized it was a natural emotion, and there was nothing she could do about it. There was no point in dwelling on it.

McReedy was gathering up wood when she returned. "I don't know about you, but I could use a hot meal."

"There's enough wood there to cook for an army," Jessie replied.

McReedy looked at the pile and smiled. "I reckon so, but we don't really know how long we'll be camped here."

For the first time Jessie realized that was true. Ki could be a few days. There was nothing to do but sit and wait. "Reckon we'll just have to make the best of it," she said aloud. There was a smile on her face that was hard to read.

"Reckon so," McReedy agreed as he smiled back.

Jessie moved closer to him.

McReedy took her in his arms and pressed his lips to hers. There was no resistance on Jessie's part. The light touch of his soft lips seemed to take her breath away, and she sighed heavily. She parted her lips and allowed his tongue to caress hers. Involuntarily she pressed her body against his, and let the warmth engulf her.

She was mildly disappointed when Chase drew away, but she managed to smile. "I guess we won't get too bored just sitting around."

"One part of me wants to scoop you right up and hold you tight. . . ." he answered.

"And the other part?" Jessie asked.

"The other part tells me there's no rush."

"True enough."

"An' maybe I should take my time."

"Do what you want, Chase."

"Would you mind if we had something to eat first?" he said somewhat hesitantly.

"A hearty appetite is a sign of a real man," she answered ambiguously.

McReedy couldn't tell if she was serious or sarcastic. "I am hungry," he said apologetically, "but I think more than anything I'd like some time for us to just talk. I hope you don't mind?"

"Far from it," Jessie answered quite honestly. "We do

have plenty of time. We have all night," she added seductively.

Chase smiled. "I don't want you to get the idea that I don't want to just hop right on you, 'cause I do. The whole day ridin' I could think of little else but you. And that's part of it. There's so much I want to know about you, Jessie. And I thought maybe we could talk some first."

"That's fine with me. There's a lot I'd like to know about you too," Jessie admitted.

They heated up some beans and put on a pot of coffee. Chase was filled with questions about Texas and didn't hesitate to ask them. He was also curious about Jessie's private affairs, and though he beat around the bush, Jessie knew what he was getting at.

"You're trying to figure out why I haven't taken a man yet, aren't you?" she said at last.

He still hemmed and hawed.

"And you're wondering if there's anyone in particular I have in mind?"

"If I knew you were so darn good at mind-reading, I could have spared myself all this pussy footing around."

"You certainly could have."

"Well?"

"Well what?"

"Well, is there anyone who's about to hitch a rope to you?"

"There are plenty that have tried, Chase. And some that I've considered as serious possibilities. But right now I just can't settle down. And there are few men who could keep pace with me."

"There's Ki."

"Ki is different. He's special."

"He must be," Chase noted. "I can hear it in your voice."

Jessie nodded. "Ki's the only man I know that doesn't try to control me."

Chase nodded. "But you don't seem absolutely positive," he remarked.

"About Ki?"

Chase nodded again.

"I'm positive. I was just thinking . . ."

"About some other man?"

Jessie laughed. "About my father. He was always looking out for me, but he never tried to control me. I reckon he knew that there was too much of him in me to have any luck at it."

"Smart man," McReedy said with a smile.

"He was."

"Was? He's passed away?"

"He was killed," she answered simply.

"What happened? Or would you rather not discuss it?"

"It's a long story, Chase. But suffice it to say he died fighting against evil. And I picked up where he left off."

"That one reason you can't settle down?"

Jessie nodded.

"There's an awful lot of evil out there to fight, Jessie. More than one woman can fight in a lifetime."

"That doesn't mean I shouldn't try."

"Nope."

"I don't go out of my way looking for it, Chase. But when I find it, I can't turn my back on it."

McReedy leaned over towards her and placed his arm around her neck. "I reckon you wouldn't be who you were if you did."

"You're very understanding, Chase."

"Maybe because you ain't my wife. Damned if I'd let my wife ride around and get shot at."

"That a fact?"

"Sure as shooting. My wife is going to sit home by the fire and take care of the kids."

"Sounds like you have it all figured out."

"Some of it."

"Just waiting for the right woman to come along?"

"I suppose so."

"And when you do you'll throw your rope around her and treat her like a prized horse."

"Now, Jessie, you're being a mite hard on me."

She didn't answer.

After a moment's pause McReedy continued. "I ain't that rigid in my thinking, Jessie." He cleared his throat. "I reckon the right woman could change my mind some. Say, a woman like you. . . ."

Jessie stood up abruptly. "While it's still warm enough, I think I'll head down to the stream and have a swim."

"I could use one myself."

"It's a free country, Mr. McReedy."

"Jessie, I hope you didn't take offense."

She shook her head. "Chase, a man like you needs a good woman. A woman who'll stay home and give him lots of children. A woman who'll stay home and take care of the family." She smiled at him. "You are planning on having lots of kids, aren't you, Chase?"

"Yup. If I can get the baby-makin' right," he said with a grin.

"You aren't so bad at it." Jessie laughed.

"I try my best, ma'am. But it's like anything else. You gotta keep working on it to get it right."

"See you down at the water," Jessie said as she turned away. There was no mistaking the twinkle in her eye.

Chase gave her a minute, then followed. By the time he got to the stream she was up to her neck in the water. Under a nearby willow was a pile of Jessie's clothes. He quickly added to the pile and went running into the stream. He hit the water with a *whooo* and splashed his way over to Jessie.

By the time he got there she was nowhere to be seen. But he felt a distinct pinch on his rear and turned quickly around.

Jessie stood there laughing. "Careful, Chase, the fish are biting."

"I'll give you biting fish," he said. Then he lunged at her.

Again she ducked under the water and came up behind him, this time wrapping her arms around him and climbing onto his back. They toppled over together.

Chase turned to grab her, but Jessie easily slipped away.

"You're harder to hold than a greased pig," he observed.

Jessie laughed and started to squeal like a pig.

"Not bad for a cowgirl," he said, and started his advance towards her. "But you're really gonna squeal when I stick you with this."

"That's what every farmboy promises, Chase."

"I don't just promise—I deliver," he said as he continued to move closer.

Jessie started to splash, jumping up and down as she did so.

Chase didn't seem to mind. In fact he rather enjoyed the sight of her firm, white breasts bobbing up and down. The cold water had her bright red nipples standing out hard and taut.

He lunged at her, grabbing her about the waist. She fell over backwards, Chase on top of her. As she pulled herself back to her feet, he was still clinging tight, but his mouth was fastened firmly on her breast. Her laughter changed to a deep sigh as he sucked on her hard bud.

But when he raised his head to attack her other breast, Jessie squirmed free. But not entirely.

Chase caught hold of her ankle and started to reel her in. Hand over hand he worked his way up her calf. By the time he reached her knee she had stopped fighting him. She spread her legs and let him slide his hand up her smooth thigh.

His other hand reached around and supported her round bottom. His hands kneaded her flesh, his fingers slowly working their way between her soft cheeks. His fingers inched along her crack into the mound of soft curly hairs, where they slipped up into her womanhood. Chase could feel her sticky nectar coating his fingers.

Jessie began to slowly gyrate her hips as Chase moved his finger in and out. "The fish are doing something they never did before," she said in a throaty whisper.

"Maybe we should get out of the water," Chase suggested.

"I wouldn't want to leave all those fish hungry," she said as she wrapped her legs around his waist.

"They do like to nibble," he answered, and with that raised her hips out of the water. He bent over and lowered his mouth to her inner thigh. He nipped at the soft skin, but did not linger there long before moving his mouth towards her mound of feminine passion. He engulfed her soft fur and ran his tongue teasingly along her moist slit.

Jessie, kicking and splashing, struggled to lift her head. Unfortunately, as Chase lifted her pelvis, her head fell under the water. "Are you trying to drown me?" she exclaimed, after spitting out a mouthful of water.

"Don't you like it, Jessie?" he asked, rather innocently, as he lowered her hips.

"Yes. Of course. But I'd wish you'd have given me some warning."

"Hold your breath," he instructed unceremoniously, then brought her body back up to his lips.

This time his tongue was more urgent, immediately finding her pleasure button. He licked at it, then sucked it into his mouth once before lowering her back into the water so she could raise her head and take another breath.

"Don't stop, Chase," she pleaded.

"I thought you might have to come up for air."

"I have a good set of lungs," she said with a smile. "I can hold my breath for some time."

"You have more than a good set of lungs, Jessie; you have the most beautiful breasts." He stretched out his hand to cup one round, firm mound. But soon slid his palm back down to her hips.

Jessie knew what to expect. "Ready whenever you are," she said excitedly.

Chase nodded and again lifted her out from the water. Jessie helped by locking her ankles around his neck. Chase had no choice, but he didn't mind. He was a willing victim as he lowered his head and let his tongue explore the folds of her petals.

For Jessie it was an exquisite feeling. Under the water every sense save one was blocked. Her eyes were closed and she couldn't see. All sounds were muffled and far away. She floated along, on a wave of pleasure, as well as the cool waters of the stream. As she held her breath she became increasingly aware of the blood pounding through her and the pleasure that was concentrated between her legs.

Regretfully, she felt the need for more air. She dug her heels into Chase's back and lifted her head out of the water. But Chase did not let go. He placed his powerful arms behind her shoulders and helped lift her up, without lowering her hips. He didn't remove his mouth. His tongue continued to caress, explore, tease.

"Oh Chase, don't stop," was all she could manage before she lowered her head back into the water.

Chase had no such inclination. He held her legs tightly around his head.

Jessie's head was swimming in a pool of ecstasy. Her blood was coursing through her. She could feel it, hear it. It was surging into her womanhood. Throbbing. And then the focus shifted. From the exterior to the interior. The pleasure seemed to grow from somewhere deep inside of her. It was no longer localized. It was taking over her whole being. She wasn't just floating, she was flying, soaring to new heights. If only her lungs could hold out. She was going to explode. Any minute. Any second.

She could feel it first in her legs as they tightened around Chase. Then her back arched involuntarily, sending more blood to her head. The pounding continued through her whole body. But she had to breathe, she had to have air. She had to fill her lungs. But most importantly she had to release.

Then a bolt shot through her body, and it was no longer a question.

She jackknifed out of the water. Her mouth let out a loud cry as her face broke through the surface.

She let her legs slip down Chase's body while she wrapped her arms around his neck. She had just brought her body up against his when she let out another gasp.

Her movement had impaled herself on his erect rod. She threw her head back as a tremor ran through her. Then, clutching him tightly, she began to pull herself up on his torso, only to let herself drop back down again.

She rode him this way till her face became red and her breath came in short gasps.

Chase took hold of Jessie's hands and unhooked them from around his neck. "Lie back and relax," he said as he lowered her into the stream.

Her body floated on the water and her legs scissored around his waist. Chase placed his hands on her hips and started to thrust into her. He maintained a steady rhythm, and Jessie soon began to feel like she was once again floating on a wave of pleasure.

She tried to move with him by flexing her legs, but the buoyancy of the water worked against her. "Maybe we should continue this in the grass?"

"I don't think I want to stop, Jessie."

"I don't want you to, either," she answered. "But I want to do more than just float. I want to make you feel wonderful, too, Chase."

"You are making me feel wonderful. And I want you to just lie there and feel it all. I want you to close your eyes and feel the sun beating down on your body, and the water cooling your skin. . . ."

"That's the least of what I feel—" she began. But the words were cut off by the thrust of his hips. Her words trailed off into a series of low moans.

"Chase, in another minute you're going to have to carry me out of the water."

He smiled at that and continued to thrust even faster. But the more vigorous efforts sent Jessie's head under water.

Chase saw what was happening and slowed his movements till he was just gently rocking inside of her.

"If we were in the grass, you wouldn't have to slow down one bit."

"There's no hurry, is there, Jessie?" he said with a smile.

For her answer she contracted her inner muscles around his turgid member. He moaned softly.

"What was that you were saying?" she asked as she squeezed him again.

He removed one hand from under her and placed it on top of her soft mound. His thumb reached out and began to massage her in smooth circles. "I was saying there was no hurry."

There was indeed no hurry, but Chase had Jessie running headlong into another climax. "I thought you might be tired of standing," she managed to mention in between gasps.

"I think we should go lie down in the grass, Jessie."

For a brief moment Jessie feared he might stop and carry her out of the water just as she was teetering on the brink. But a second later her worries were put to rest—first by his words, then by his actions.

"It'll feel awfully nice to lie on top of you," Chase started to say. "But I don't think we'll stop just yet."

That quickly soothed her concern. Chase increased the pressure of his thumb, and his strokes came harder and faster. There was no turning back.

She let out a small gasp, and her body shuddered violently.

Jessie didn't realize until it was too late that Chase had slipped out from her. "We could have made it out together," she said as he scooped her up and carried her out of the water.

"It's faster this way," he told her. "It'll only be a minute."

He was true to his word.

Jessie felt the grass under her. Then, almost instantly, she felt Chase push into her. She spread her legs wide and tilted her pelvis forward.

"It feels good to have something solid under me," she said as she met his every thrust.

Chase laughed. "I didn't think it could feel any better," he said in a low growl. Then he lowered his head to her breasts.

Jessie started to run her fingers through his hair as his mouth sucked hungrily at her buds.

He continued to ride her, his thrusts becoming increasingly more urgent.

Jessie lifted her legs high into the air, and took hold of his muscular rear end.

"Is this the same woman that had to be carried from the water weak and exhausted?"

"I don't know why, but I feel totally revived." She punctuated her remark with another squeeze of her inner muscles.

"If you do that again, Jessie, I'm going to be the one weak and exhausted."

Jessie smiled and answered the only way she knew how —with another squeeze. She could feel Chase's muscles stiffen. She locked her legs around his waist and tried to meld her body against his. She matched his every movement, his every thrust. And when she felt the feeling start to overtake her again, she clamped down hard. She engulfed his hard rod with every inch of her muscles, and wouldn't let go.

"It feels so good," he managed to say in between gasps.

Jessie began to run her fingers up and down his back. She could feel him shudder.

"I can't hold back, Jessie," he groaned.

"I don't want you to, Chase." She squeezed him for the last time.

He thrust hard; then his body went rigid. She felt the

explosion deep inside of her, the contractions that seemed never to end.

Then she let out a deep groan as her body shook uncontrollably with another orgasm.

When she opened her eyes Chase's head was nestled between her breasts. The sun had already set.

Chapter 9

Ki did a quick job of saddling his horse. But in the few minutes it took, Chen's rig moved out of sight.

It was not a serious problem. Chen was probably heading back to the Dobson house, and although Ki did not know the exact location, he knew the general direction to go. He pushed his horse into a well-placed trot and started down the road.

A mile out of town he caught sight of the rig. Ki realized later that if he had slowed his horse then, it would have been much easier. But as he was eager to speak with Chen, he kept the animal in a trot.

Chen suddenly became aware of the horseman chasing him and snapped his two-horse team into a full-speed gallop.

The wagon began to pull ahead and Ki had to push his horse to keep up. But the distance began to close rapidly. The wagon team, initially faster, could not sustain the gallop for any length of time.

Ki pulled his horse alongside the speeding wagon and shouted for Chen to rein in. The Chinaman looked at Ki oddly, but continued to whip his team forward.

Ki was considering jumping from his saddle into the wagon, where he could overpower Chen and bring the wagon to a stop. But he decided against it. Chen must have taken flight to avoid being robbed, thinking Ki was a highwayman. To have to subdue the Chinaman by force would create more suspicion and make Ki's job harder. Ultimately, Ki needed Chen as a friend.

He squeezed a little more speed from his mount and drew up alongside the team. He leaned over, grabbed hold of the lead horse's bit, and pulled back. The team started to slow, but Ki was in a precarious situation. His own horse shied away from running that close to the wagon team, and only Ki's strength—his firm hold of the bit and his strong pull on his own horse's reins—kept him from falling in between the two.

Chen jerked on the leads and the wagon team turned sharply. Ki was surprised at the quickness with which the team reacted; he was suddenly in a position that demanded he let go of the bridle.

Ki also had the ability to react quickly, and he did so. He chose not to let go of the wagon's harness. Instead, he slipped his feet from the stirrups of his own horse, and pushed out of his saddle.

An instant later he was sitting astride the left horse of the wagon team. The change of mounts was done in one fluid motion that belied the deadly danger of the maneuver. One false move, one slight misjudgment, and Ki would have been trampled by the hooves of the charging team. If by some miraculous chance he'd avoided the horses, the wagon would certainly have run him over and ground him into a bloody pulp. But Ki had left no room for miscalculation. He knew that his own life, and often the lives of others, depended on accuracy and speed. He did these acrobatics as a matter of second nature.

From his new position he easily grabbed hold of the lead lines and pulled the team to a stop.

But when he turned around, Chen was already hopping down from the wagon and running down the road.

"I mean you no harm," Ki yelled, then jumped down and took off after him.

It was during the short pursuit that Ki noticed that Chen was tall and long-legged. For a moment, Ki thought the man, like himself, came from mixed parentage.

Thirty yards later Ki dove at the man's feet, bringing him down with a solid thud. Ki regretted having to use force, but there was no other choice. It was not feasible to continue running until Chen grew tired.

Ki picked himself up. Chen lay face down on the ground. "You can stand up," Ki said. "I mean you no harm."

Chen slowly rose to his knees, all the time keeping his back to Ki. Then he stood up and turned around quickly, a small dagger in his hand.

"I am not afraid to die," he said. "Can you say the same?" His eyes narrowed. "You are not Chinese," he observed.

Ki shook his head. "No."

"*Jibon-ren,*" he spat out.

Ki nodded. "I am half Japanese, half American."

"When does the Tong send out dogs to do its dirty work?" Chen asked.

"The Tong has not sent me, and I mean you no harm."

It was obvious the Chinaman did not believe him. He stood on his guard, his dagger at the ready.

"If I wanted to kill you, why would I bother to stop the wagon?" Ki asked.

Chen did not hesitate. "You wear no gun."

"Isn't that unusual for a Tong man?"

"No. They do not need guns to kill."

Ki smiled and slipped his hand into his vest pocket. He pulled out a *shuriken*. Chen stiffened visibly. "I see you know what this is."

Chen nodded.

"Then watch," commanded Ki. "That tree over there . . ." His eyes were on a scrub oak fifteen yards away. With a flick of his wrist he sent the *shuriken* flying. A second later it dug into the bark of the tree. "If I wished it, you would be long dead."

Chen realized there was truth to the statement. But he was still wary. "Then what do you want from me?"

Ki didn't answer immediately. He first wanted to know about Chen's curious behavior. "Why did you think I was sent by the Tong?"

Chen shrugged. "In town they told me a countryman of mine was looking for me. They did not know who, or why."

"And you immediately thought—"

"No relative would come visit," Chen cut him short.

"You have had trouble with the Tong before?"

Chen did not answer.

"I am no friend of the Tong, Chen. I have fought them myself. If you are in trouble, maybe I can help."

Chen shook his head. "No one can help. One cannot fight the Tong. One can only run."

Ki felt otherwise, but he did not try to convince Chen. He was starting to get an idea. "The Tong is after you?" he asked to be sure.

"It is possible," Chen answered.

"Why?"

"It does not matter," he said at first. Then for a moment he struggled for the right word. "There is a reason, it is hard to explain. I have heard men use the word 'vendetta.'"

Ki nodded. "I understand. And if I knew you were here, it is possible the Tong knows it as well."

"I am afraid that is so," Chen admitted.

"Then you must keep running."

Chen did not respond and Ki continued. "It must take a great deal of money to run from place to place?"

Chen flashed a smile that had no humor in it. "Yes," he said simply.

"Where will you go?" Ki asked. "Perhaps we can help each other," he suggested when no answer was forthcoming.

"Perhaps."

"I need to learn about Delbert Dobson. You need money and a place to go, a place where there will be a job for you."

When Chen nodded his head, Ki told him the rest of the plan.

The Chinaman thought it over. "How do I know I can trust you?"

"Why would I try to deceive you?" Ki asked.

"I cannot say."

Ki smiled. "Do you have a better plan?"

"No."

Ki dug into his pocket and pulled out a handful of rolled bills. "There is nothing deceitful about this money. It is yours in addition to everything else I have promised."

Chen had no choice. He agreed to the plan, and took the money. Ki gave him his horse, and sped him on his way.

Riding along in Chen's wagon, Ki began to have second thoughts. Mainly he was concerned about Jessie. She would have no idea what had happened to him, and Ki did not foresee getting the opportunity to send word to her. Ki never liked to worry her needlessly, but this time he had no choice. A door had opened, and he had taken it.

He thought about sending a message with Chen, but once the Chinaman had agreed to the plan, Ki did not want to delay him further. The sooner Chen left the better.

By the time he returned into the road that led to the Dobson House, Ki had worked out the last few pieces of his story. He didn't think there would be any problem pulling off the masquerade; he just wasn't sure that it would be worth the effort. But as he came in sight of the house, he realized that it was his best chance.

The Dobson house was an impressive stone structure, better described as a mansion. Its turrets, arches, and bay windows owed much to European design, while its large wraparound porch was very Western in style. But as impressive as the house was, its location was even more inspiring. It was built on the shore of a small lake that was nestled in between two mountains. Ki could count a half-dozen streams that cascaded down the peaks into the lake.

For a brief moment Ki no longer wondered why Dobson had settled here in Waterville. One could search far and wide and not find a spot more beautiful than this. He doubted Helena had anything to match it. A man with money could build what he wished, but no amount of wealth could create scenery like this.

It complicated matters to think that maybe there was nothing suspicious about Dobson living in Waterville. But that was what Ki was here to find out.

He had just pulled into the yard when a stable hand came out of the barn. "What the hell happened to Chen, and who the hell are you?" he demanded.

"Chen had to go away. My name is Ki. I have come to replace him."

"Like hell you have," the man barked. He wasn't much over twenty, and his position as stable hand didn't give him much authority. But he was high enough to talk down to the Chinese help. Ki took his remark to be one of surprise rather than belligerence. "Best bring that rig around back," he continued, "and I'll get the boss."

Ki did as he was told. He was wondering whether "the boss" referred to Dobson or the foreman. He had his answer when the stable hand returned with a hardened cowpuncher in his late thirties. The man looked the part of foreman, from the leathery face and dirty work clothes to the swagger of authority with which he moved. There was only one odd thing—the Peacemaker that hung on his hip. Out on the range cowmen always wore their guns, but unless the ranch was located in Indian country, it was unusual to see a man walk around the yard packing an iron. Ki, though, did not want to leap to any conclusions. It was curious, but not damning.

"That's a Dobson rig you're riding, boy. And those are Dobson supplies," the foreman said as he pointed to the back of the wagon.

"And I hope to be a Dobson employee," Ki said calmly.

The foreman let out a laugh. "We got more Chinee than we need."

Ki remained silent. He did not want to antagonize the man.

"Where's that good-for-nothing Chen?" the foreman asked.

"He had to go back to San Francisco. His father is ill."

"And who are you?"

"My name is Ki. I am a friend of Chen's, a friend of his family. I brought the news to him. Chen left at once, and I have come to replace him." Ki lowered his head slightly. "That is, if it is all right with you."

"You ever work as a houseboy before?"

"Yes."

"I reckon we'll give you a try. You do as you're told and there'll be no problem. Savvy?"

Ki nodded. "Yes, sir."

The foreman turned to the stable hand. "Hank, show him where to put those things. Then point him to his room. I'll go tell Mr. Dobson." Without even a look at Ki he entered the house.

Ki carried the kitchen supplies into the pantry. There he met Juanita, and his biggest worry came to an end. Ki had not bothered to ask Chen if there was a cook, and for a while Ki became concerned that meals were the China-man's responsibility. It wasn't that Ki couldn't cook; he was in fact quite a good cook, but the time needed to prepare meals would drastically cut down his ability to snoop around. Ki wouldn't be able to investigate much if he spent most of his day in the kitchen. So he was rather happy to meet the Spanish woman. The cook returned his genuine smile with a warm, friendly greeting of her own. Ki couldn't help notice that though Juanita's hair was streaked with gray she was still an attractive woman.

Juanita showed Ki around the house and instructed him on his duties. He was to pick up goods from town, drive Mr. Dobson or other guests around in the buggy, and serve meals. Cleaning, washing, and ironing were duties that were shared between the two of them. Ki didn't expect to have any difficulties carrying out his responsibilities.

It was dinnertime before he met Delbert Dobson. Ki was mildly surprised. First, he had expected an older man. Dobson was a fit-looking man in his mid-forties. He had a full head of shiny, black hair, slicked back, and a well-groomed handlebar mustache. Though he didn't stand very tall and didn't appear to have any great strength, there was no fat on his frame.

The other surprise sat next to Dobson. This was a young lady of exceptional beauty. She was fair-skinned, blue-eyed, and blond. Her long hair was pinned on top of her head and exposed a slender neck. She had delicate features, a thin nose, and narrow lips. But for all her beauty, Ki couldn't help notice a dull, bored expression in her eyes.

Throughout the meal Dobson kept referring to her as "dear." Ki didn't remember her speaking much at all. He assumed it was a typical case of a young girl marrying an older man for his money, power, and position. She could have done much worse. Dobson was still a virile man. Yet the woman looked unhappy. Ki suspected it had to do with living out in the wilds of nowhere. As ideal as it was, she no doubt would have preferred to remain back East. She looked like she would have been much happier among the society women of Baltimore than the mountains and streams of Montana.

But that was not the last of the surprises. As he started to bring out the coffee, Juanita handed him one cup of tea. "She never touches coffee," the cook said simply. "She considers it unladylike." There was a drop of mockery in her voice.

"I'll remember that," Ki said. "Do I bring Mrs. Dobson milk or sugar?" he started to ask, but he didn't get an answer. The cook was too busy laughing.

"'Mrs. Dobson,' that is a funny thought," she said when

99

her laugh had died down to a chuckle. "I suppose you have no way of knowing."

Ki already had a good idea of his mistake, but he asked anyway. "Knowing what?"

"That is his daughter, Sylvia."

Ki's room was a small chamber tucked behind the pantry. He lay on his cot till he thought everyone was asleep, then silently went to Dobson's study. He lit the lamp and began searching through the large roll-top desk. The fact that none of the drawers was locked was a good indication that Ki would find nothing important. But it was a good place to begin.

Though he didn't realize its significance, Ki did find something curious—a government census of the Montana Territory. He put it back in the drawer and went to find the safe. It was hidden behind a large oil painting of what Ki took to be Grand-dad Dobson.

In an empty house, the safe would not present any problem, but there was no way Ki could get into it now without waking up everyone. He replaced the portrait and had started for the door when he thought he heard footsteps outside in the hall. He looked quickly for a place to hide, and found none that was satisfactory. He might have tried to conceal himself under the desk, or behind the curtain if it were not for the lamp. The lamp, even when doused, would give off the unmistakable scent of burning oil. The odor would be a dead giveaway that someone was in the room. No matter where Ki tried to hide, a simple search would find him. Concealment was not an viable option.

He was about to rush to the door and wait behind it for the person to enter. A quick *shuto-uchi,* a knife-hand strike to the back of the neck, would drop the person where he stood, but chances were that Ki, the newcomer, would be the first suspect. Even if no one suspected him, the household would be on its guard, something Ki did not want.

Time and alternatives were running out when Ki slid quickly into the desk chair. He put a sheet of paper in front of him then grabbed the quill pen just as the door opened.

"I suppose you have a good reason for being here?" a soft voice demanded.

Ki feigned surprise and looked up.

It was Sylvia Dobson. "Is there a reason why I shouldn't yell for my father this instant?"

The fact that she had not already done so was a good sign. He was prepared to act dumb and try to stammer his way out of this, but something in the girl's manner told him to be direct. "Please do not," Ki said simply.

"Then what the hell are you doing here?"

"I realized that I had not told anyone that I was staying on here in Waterville."

"So . . . ?"

"I came here to write a letter to my family. In my room there was no paper or pen. I also did not wish to take out time from my work day."

"How considerate of you," Sylvia said as she sat down. She wrapped her nightgown around her as she did so, but a corner of her slim calf peeked out from under the white silk.

"I want to do my best," Ki answered.

Sylvia studied Ki closely. "You are a cousin of Chen's?"

Ki shook his head. "We are not related."

"Well, at least you're honest."

"Did you know for a fact that Chen had no cousins?" Ki said with a smile.

"No. But I would find it hard to accept that a Chinese man would have a Japanese cousin. Or are you only part Japanese?"

Ki nodded. "A very good observation."

"I can also observe that you are a bit more educated than our former houseboy."

"Because a man has problems expressing himself in a foreign language does not mean he is uneducated."

"I see you have no problem," she observed dryly.

"I am well trained," Ki agreed.

Her eyes narrowed. "Perhaps too well trained to be a houseboy."

Ki laughed, and though he appeared to be casual, he was anything but. He realized he had better answer very carefully. "Personally, I would agree with you, Miss Sylvia, but unfortunately, others do not."

"You also seem very well bred."

Ki smiled. "Although I am half American, to most who offer employment, I am a heathen. I take what I can get. That is how I know Chen. We both worked on the Central Pacific." Ki knew he was going out on a limb, but he thought it better to answer the question before she asked it. And he was positive she would ask it next.

"I didn't know he worked on the railroad."

Ki nodded, and played it calm. "It is nothing for a man to be proud of."

Sylvia smiled coldly. "No, I suppose there is no pride in being a coolie."

"We are not all fortunate enough to be born into rich families," he said sharply.

Sylvia's long, blond hair was hanging freely; she gave it a toss, and smiled at Ki. "There are those who are born to be pampered and those who are born to do the pampering. We need men like you and Chen," she said coldly. "We need you to serve us and wait on us, and see to our every need."

"The only thing you need is a good spanking," Ki told her. He started to get up.

"Wait a minute," she snapped. "I'm not through with you yet."

"Maybe I'm through with you."

"As long as you're in this house, you'll do as I say." Her voice was soft and sweet, but she was fooling no one.

Ki looked at her. "As long as *I* am in this house," he said. From his tone it was understood that his term of employment could be terminated momentarily.

Sylvia went to the door, blocking the exit with her body. Slowly she undid her robe and the top buttons of her nightgown. Her breasts, small and milk-white, jutted out freely. "If I scream, they'll be in here in a minute. They'll take one look at me, then string you up from the nearest tree."

Ki did not answer. He took another step to the door.

"If you doubt it, take another step," she threatened.

Ki didn't doubt it at all. But he sensed from Sylvia's hesitation that she was bluffing. But she had soft skin, pink nipples, and long, shapely legs, and Ki considered giving her just what she needed.

He took another step and realized that he had guessed wrong. Though not entirely. She didn't scream. She did something more deadly. From her robe pocket she pulled a small two-shot derringer.

"If a rope doesn't scare you, maybe this will."

Ki stood motionless.

"If you're thinking I don't know how to use it, try me."

"It doesn't take much knowledge to know how to pull a trigger, Miss Sylvia."

Sylvia gave a dry chuckle. "I like my animals to have spunk. It's a good trait in a horse, especially a stallion."

"Too much spirit, and one can get kicked in the head," Ki cautioned.

Sylvia raised the derringer.

Ki tensed, ready to strike.

With her other hand Sylvia slid her hand up her thigh, pulling aside her silk nightgown and exposing a curly thatch of light brown hair. She let her fingers roam through her bush as she raised her gown even higher.

She smiled wickedly at Ki. "Down on your knees!"

★

Chapter 10

Ki did as he was told.

Sylvia moved towards him and straddled his face, slowly lowering her body onto his lips. "Do me right," she demanded, "or else . . ."

She didn't finish her sentence, but there was no misunderstanding the derringer that pressed lightly against the back of his head. There was no question in Ki's mind what would happen if he failed to perform to Sylvia's satisfaction.

At first he licked at her gently. He was uninterested, and did so only as a matter of necessity. It was a purely mechanical action. But as her warm thighs pressed against his cheeks and the musky aroma of her body filled his head, his desire increased. Ki raised his arms and cupped her round buttocks in his hands, pulling her closer to him. His mouth engulfed her soft mound while his fingers lightly caressed the back of her thighs.

Sylvia started to moan softly and rocked her body to the movement of Ki's tongue.

"Lick my juice," she said in a raspy voice. "Suck every drop," she commanded in between heavy breaths.

Sylvia was not being flippant; she was in a state of heavy arousal, and warm, sticky moisture flowed copiously from her depths. Ki's face was totally coated, and he licked hungrily, like a grizzly with a honeycomb.

Sylvia's legs started to flex, and she began to grind her soft mound into Ki's face. Her hands took hold of his head and pressed it hard against her body.

Ki increased the pressure against her swollen pleasure bud, and Sylvia let out a gasp. "You're the best!" she exclaimed, and started to shudder.

Ki could feel her body tremble. He started to withdraw his head. Sylvia tried to force it back against her pouting womanhood, but Ki's head couldn't be forced.

"Don't stop now, you bastard," she pleaded.

Ki had no intention of stopping, at least not totally. He flicked his tongue at her ever so lightly. At the touch of it she shuddered again. Ki pulled back and once more ran his tongue slowly over her dripping gash.

"Lick it! Lick it!" she gasped, and tried to grind against his face.

But the harder she tried to force herself against Ki, the further he pulled back. But he never pulled back more than a tongue's length. He continued to flick the tip of his tongue over her sensitive folds.

"Please, don't tease me any longer," she whimpered. Her tone, though still insistent, no longer held the bark of her earlier commands.

Ki smiled to himself and continued to administer to her in slow, steady movements. He pressed his tongue along the length of her womanhood, the way a horse licks at a salt block.

"Damn!" Sylvia said suddenly and pushed Ki away.

She strode over to the desk and threw herself face down over it. Her nightgown was high up on her back. She reached behind her and pulled apart her soft white buns. "Give it to me, now!" The urgency and demand was back in her voice.

Ki stood up and moved closer to her. He ran his fingers lightly over her soft, rounded flesh, and though his organ was fully erect and throbbing hard he ignored her plea.

"Can't you see how ready I am for you?" she said breathlessly.

Ki could in fact see her deep scarlet lips, wet and puckering. He ran a finger lightly over her mound.

Sylvia reached behind her and felt for his tool. She gasped when she found it. "You're so hard. You must want it too. What are you waiting for?"

Ki did not answer. He continued to run his finger through her moist curls.

"Please, Ki, please," she said as she squeezed his hard shaft. "I want you."

Ki paid no attention, though he did realize that that was the first time she had called him by name.

Sylvia let out a sob. "I need you, Ki. I do. Please!" she begged, as she thrust out her hips and tried to rub her backside against his hard pole.

Ki let her rub her body against his.

"Ki, I'm sorry I talked to you like that. Truly I am. Don't punish me any longer. I'll be a good girl. Honest. I'll be a good girl, you'll see."

Ki undid his pants, and his massive organ popped free.

"Oh yes, Ki," she said as her hand started to stroke it. "I'll be a good girl, I will."

Ki took hold of her hips and slowly guided himself into her waiting tunnel. Then he pushed hard into her. She was indeed sopping wet, and he slid all the way to the hilt.

Sylvia let out a loud gasp, and arched her back to meet his thrust. "Yes, oh yes!"

She started to buck wildly, moving her hips in every which direction.

"Give it to me, give it to me," she started to cry as she wriggled around on his erect shaft.

Ki feared her voice would wake the house, and he quickly clasped his hand over her mouth.

Holding her mouth like that brought her head back and restricted many of her wild movements much like the bit and bridle of a horse. It also allowed Ki to thrust deeply into her. Which he did. Repeatedly.

Sylvia let out a small cry and began to rock her hips in unison with Ki's thrusts.

Ki could feel her excitement growing. She seemed infinitely warmer and wetter. He could feel her body beginning to tense, yearning for release. He could also feel his own excitement growing. It wouldn't be long before she climaxed, and her spasms would no doubt send him over the edge to release with her. He started to move his hips faster, plunging deeper. . . .

They both heard it together—the door opening.

Ki withdrew quickly.

Sylvia hurried to cover herself, dropping her nightgown back in place. But there was no hiding it. They had been caught.

She turned quickly to see Juanita standing in the doorway.

Sylvia seemed to act almost instinctively. The derringer was still in her hand, and she brought it up to shoulder height, taking only a second to aim before firing.

Ki saw the movement out of the corner of his eye and brought his hand down hard on Sylvia's wrist. Only his quickness saved the housekeeper's life.

The bullet bit into the floor, just inches from Juanita's feet.

For a moment Ki stared at Sylvia. He couldn't believe she had tried to kill Juanita. Then he realized that to the spoiled Sylvia, her honor and reputation were more important than another's life. She would sooner commit murder than live with the shame of being caught in a compromising position with Ki, a lowly houseboy. Ki was repulsed and angered.

Deliberately he slapped Sylvia's face. Hard.

There were tears in her eyes but she didn't cry out. Her face was deeply flushed, almost to a shade of crimson.

Ki understood the significance of his act. It wasn't bad enough to be caught in a carnal embrace; now she had to suffer the humiliation of being slapped.

She looked Ki in the eye, and without a word or a look to Juanita, lifted her robe and stormed out of the room.

Only then did Ki realize he was standing with his pants around his ankles, his tool totally exposed and fully erect. He fumbled getting his pants up.

Juanita suddenly laughed. "Do not feel embarrassment, señor Ki." Her eyes softened. "There is no shame in your manhood."

He was about to answer when they heard heavy steps in the hall.

Ki rushed to the window and opened it.

A moment later Delbert Dobson, gun in hand, entered the room.

"What's going on?" he demanded. "Was that a shot I heard?"

Ki turned from the open window. "Your daughter must have seen something. . . ." Ki began.

Dobson nodded. "I saw her rushing up the steps. . . ."

"Perhaps a wolf moving out there," Ki said, pointing out the window.

"We don't have many wolves around here," Dobson answered coldly.

Ki shrugged.

"Could have been a coyote," Dobson remarked. "Sometimes they come prowling around the house."

Juanita chuckled. "That'll be the last time that coyote comes pokin' around in here."

Dobson smiled. "I trust you're right, Juanita. Close up that window Ki, and let's all get back to bed." He started to leave, then stopped to ask one last question. "What was my daughter doing down here in the first place?" He looked from Ki to Juanita and smiled. "A rhetorical question," he assured them. "But thank you both for coming to her aid so quickly. Good night." With that he left the room and went back upstairs.

Ki turned to Juanita. "Are there any coffee grounds?" he asked.

She seemed confused, but she nodded. "Right outside the kitchen door, but why?"

"I'm lucky he believed me," Ki answered.

Juanita agreed. "If he knew the truth, *aye caramba*. . . ."

Ki laughed. "And I want to make sure he doesn't learn the truth."

"Do not worry about the *señorita*. I think she will die before letting on what has happened."

"I'm not worried about Sylvia," Ki assured her. "Wait here and watch," he said, then left for the kitchen door.

A moment later he returned, holding something in his cupped palm. He bent down at Juanita's feet and continued his explanation. "I don't want Dobson sitting at his desk tomorrow and wondering what this fresh gouge in his floor is."

"*Dios mío,*" she exclaimed.

Ki pulled a *shuriken* out of his pocket and used the sharp tip to dig out the small bullet from the floorboard. Then he darkened the freshly splintered wood with the coffee grounds. It filled the small hole and turned the light wood into a darker stain. He stood up and smiled. "It's not a perfect match, but unless one is looking for it, it won't be noticed."

He dropped his throwing star back into his pocket, then handed Juanita the small piece of lead. "A souvenir," he said.

"Not every woman is fortunate enough to be given the bullet that was meant to kill her. A very precious gift," she said sincerely. "A gift that must be repaid."

"There is no need," Ki said with a smile.

She smiled back at him. "But I think there is. It was most rude of me to interrupt. And before you were completed." There was genuine concern in her voice.

"It was not as enjoyable as it seemed," Ki said simply.

Juanita chuckled. "You will not have me believe that, *señor*. You were sticking out like a stallion. *Muy grande . . .*"

She moved closer to him and lowered her voice slightly. "A man does not like to be unsatisfied. It is not good." She reached for his tool and began to rub it through his loose-fitting pants. "What was it *señor* Dobson has said? 'We should all go back to bed,' yes?"

Juanita's bed was soft and warm. So was she. She wrapped her arms around Ki and pressed him against her full breasts as he lay between her spread legs. They moved together

111

slowly, Juanita rolling her hips as Ki slid his shaft in and out of her.

She didn't have the youthful zeal of Sylvia, but she had the experience of age. She didn't wriggle and buck in a frantic passion; she moved deliberately, with Ki, to increase both their pleasure.

"Yes, my lover," she whispered in his ear. "Feel good. Feel good like you make Juanita feel." She licked at his ear, then nibbled on his earlobe.

Involuntarily Ki picked up his rhythm, thrusting with long, powerful strokes. Juanita met his every move, her hips raising high off the bed. There was a soft smack every time their bodies met. The sound, the feel of her skin, the warmth around his shaft, all had Ki in a state of ecstasy.

He reached under her, grabbed Juanita's fleshy buttocks, and began to knead her bottom.

She groaned loudly, then grabbed Ki's muscular buns, digging her nails into his skin. Like spurs on a horse, they urged Ki on faster.

"I can't last any longer," she panted. "You are driving me *loco*."

"Good," Ki said with a smile.

"I'll lose my head. I might scream."

Ki lowered his mouth to hers. His lips pressed lightly against hers as he continued to pump in and out of her. Although it was hardly audible they could still sense the guttural sounds Juanita was making deep inside her throat. They were timed to his every thrust.

He changed his pace, and her moaning changed. He began to rock his hips slowly and gently, and her cries became lower. He removed his mouth from hers and began to trace her lips with the tip of his tongue. Her cries were silent now, but her breath started coming in deep gasps. Ki knew she was close. His slow movements picked up speed, his gentle gyrations turned into a deep shafting.

Juanita threw her head back and opened her mouth wide. Ki lowered his mouth and sucked on her red, thick lower lip. She started to tremble, and Ki pressed his lips to hers.

Juanita wrapped her arms around Ki's shoulders and clung tightly to him. Her back arched and she tried to press every inch of her body against Ki.

Ki shoved his tongue deep into her mouth, and Juanita's body stiffened, but only for a moment. She let out a stifled cry, and then her body was wracked with convulsions.

She held Ki tightly, and after a moment seemed to relax. But her inner muscles did anything but. They continued to flex against his hard shaft, refusing to let up.

"It's never been this strong," Juanita gasped in surprise. "Will it ever stop?"

Ki didn't know, but he was hoping it never would. Her grip was fantastic and every movement sent a chill up his spine. His pleasure increased and spread. It was no longer centered in the nerves of his throbbing manhood, but spread outward, engulfing his whole being. He thrust his tool deeply into Juanita's wet sheath, but felt as if his whole body was sliding in and out of her. He was lost in a sea of sensation, nearly out of control as he hovered on the verge of explosion.

And still Juanita's body trembled and shook. "Never this long," she gasped again. "Make it stop, *señor*. Only you can make it stop."

"I don't want it to stop, Juanita. It feels too good."

"Make it stop," she repeated. "Shoot inside of me. Now, Ki. Now."

Ki had no choice. He was beyond the point of control.

But Juanita was taking no chances. She reached behind Ki and grabbed hold of his large sack.

The touch of her fingers sent Ki over the edge. With powerful contractions, he fired deep inside of her.

Juanita's eyes went wide, and her body stiffened again. She let out a long, slow moan. It seemed to last forever, and when it stopped she lay there quietly.

Ki slid out from her and lay by her side.

Juanita kissed Ki on the cheek. "I owe you for more than my life," she said softly. "To have lived but never have experienced such as this would have been the bigger shame. But now I am a fulfilled woman."

"You are a beautiful woman, Juanita."

"I will die happy," she said with a twinkle in her eye.

"Not soon I hope."

"Why?" she asked cunningly. "You wish to make more love to Juanita?"

Ki nodded. "Many more times," he said with a smile.

"An old woman like me, when you can have someone young and pretty like *la señorita* . . ."

Ki didn't let her finish. "You have given me great pleasure, Juanita."

"And I can see you wish to be pleasured again," she said as she looked down at his still hard manhood.

She did not wait for an answer. She slid down and engulfed his rod with her warm, wet mouth. Her head moved up and down, and soon she was relaxed enough to take the full length of his shaft.

Ki let out a moan.

Juanita raised her head for a moment. "Now it is my turn to make you feel good," she said as she lowered her lips back to his tumescent manhood.

Ki started to move his hips, at first in small movements,

then, at Juanita's urging, in fuller, longer strokes, till his rod slid deeply into her throat.

Juanita used her mouth the way she had used her body and Ki could feel the pressure building within his loins once more.

It was a big disappointment when Juanita stopped and lay down on her back. "I am sorry, Ki," she explained. "You are too big for my little mouth. And I do not wish to hurt you."

"It didn't hurt," Ki assured her.

"I am afraid my jaw will grow tired, and my teeth will bite down on you." As she said this she pressed her large breasts together. "Are they not inviting?" she asked.

Ki leaned over and took her large brown nipple in his mouth. He sucked on it hungrily and felt it grow hard.

Meanwhile Juanita took hold of his shaft and stroked it with a light but steady grip.

Ki let his tongue dance over to her other breast and proceeded to suck that dark bud. It too stiffened in his mouth.

Ki was yearning to bury his shaft back in her warm sheath. He started to roll on top of her, but her hold tightened around his organ.

"I am too sore, Ki. I am not used to such a vigorous riding." Then she smiled "But I do not wish to disappoint you." Holding his shaft she guided him up to her breasts.

"They will please you, will they not?" she asked coyly.

Ki straddled her stomach, his rod falling into the cleavage between her full, ripe breasts.

Juanita pressed her breasts together and her flesh swallowed up most of his shaft. Slowly she started to massage her breasts. "It feels nice, yes, Ki?"

"Very nice," he answered. The warmth and softness of her bosom had a different feel from her moist tunnel, or her wet, seductive mouth, but it was going to elicit the same results.

Juanita must have sensed his growing excitement. She let go of her breasts, took hold of Ki's hands, and placed them on her mounds.

He rubbed her large nipples while holding her breasts around his hard shaft. He began pumping his hips, watching his manhood slide between her soft globes.

Juanita's hand found the base of his organ and started to squeeze. "Do not hold back," she urged. Then she raised her head and her tongue sought the crimson tip of his manhood, which was peeking out from between her soft mounds.

It only took one flick of her tongue before Ki splashed his seed all over her face and neck.

"Muchas gracias, señor," Juanita said with a smile.

"The pleasure was all mine," Ki answered honestly, as he lay down next to her.

"You do not have to leave," Juanita said softly.

Ki wasn't sure if it was an invitation or a question. It didn't matter. He wasn't going anywhere. He placed his arm around her, and pulled her close.

Juanita nestled against his strong shoulders and soon drifted off to sleep.

The next day was like any other. Juanita did her chores, as did Ki. Dobson spent much of the day in his study, but didn't find the nicked floorboard. Sylvia was not at breakfast, but she was at the dinner table. She seemed a little sullen, and didn't speak much. She totally avoided looking at Ki and Juanita, but there was nothing unusual about that. Until their meeting in the study, Sylvia had not said one word to Ki. So all in all the incident the night before had changed little. Things were back to normal.

And that bothered Ki. He had not come to the Dobson house to work as a houseboy, or for that matter to make love to an aging but still sensuous Spanish *señorita*. He had come looking for answers, and he was finding damn few. For a moment he considered the possibility that there was nothing crooked about Delbert Dobson, that perhaps it was some underling, a second in command, who was masterminding the swindle.

Ki had no reason to believe or disbelieve that. The fact was, he had little proof of anything. He was starting to wonder if his plan of working as a houseboy made any sense. It did bring him into the house, which initially seemed like a good idea, but now, since he had uncovered nothing, it only served to limit his freedom of movement.

Perhaps his time would be better spent in the saloon, keeping his eyes and ears open. Or maybe he should spend his days following the foreman. A lackey running an errand often exposed more of the scheme than the boss, who would go to great lengths to keep his hands clean.

Then Ki thought about the safe in the study. Maybe all the answers were in there. It would be difficult to break into the safe and still maintain his cover as an innocent houseboy. It was possible, but unless the right opportunity presented itself, the chances of success were slim. It would, in essence, take an empty house—an unlikely proposition at best. The other alternative would be to blow the safe and hightail it out of there. If Ki found what he was looking for, it would be worth the risk, but if he came up emptyhanded it would do more harm than good. Dobson would realize that someone was onto him, or at least was suspicious of his activities. Forewarned, he could take immediate action to cover his trail. Dobson, if he was scared enough, might even put all his dealings into good order, and then it would be nearly impossible to expose the

117

swindle. That was a move Ki did not want to push Dobson into. As long as Dobson remained ignorant, there was a chance to catch him.

So for now Ki was stuck as a houseboy. Juanita made the job far from boring. In fact, Ki often found himself thinking about her. There were worse positions to be in, Ki thought with a smile.

Maybe he was just being impatient. A vulture wouldn't find a fresh kill every day, but if one waited long enough, eventually one would catch the buzzard in the act. Perhaps Ki just had to wait.

★

Chapter 11

"You look like a caged polecat," Chase remarked.

"Restless?" Jessie asked.

Chase nodded. "And then some." He was sitting comfortably under a willow tree. "I'm getting a mite tired of watching you pace back and forth."

"I don't like waiting," Jessie answered, as she continued to walk along the edge of the stream.

"It's only been two days. And a very enjoyable two days, I might add."

"I didn't come out here to enjoy myself," Jessie said sharply.

"I didn't say you did," Chase answered calmly, but he was obviously hurt.

"I'm sorry I snapped, Chase."

He smiled. "Just like a caged polecat," he repeated.

"I think I'm also a little worried about Ki."

"You said he could take care of himself."

"He can."

119

"Then stop worrying."

"I just wish he would have sent word back," Jessie said.

"How? Western Union?"

"I think Ki would have found something by now."

"There's no telling, Jessie."

"He might have gotten into some sort of trouble."

"He's one tough hombre," Chase repeated.

"That doesn't mean he won't get into a tight spot."

"Jessie, I doubt he's in serious trouble."

"We're all mortal."

"And there's nothing you or I can do about it. Now sit down and watch the sun set."

Jessie smiled. "I reckon I am acting a little crazy." She sat down next to him. "It's just that I feel best when I'm doing something. I just hate to sit idle and watch things take their course."

"Sometimes you have no choice."

"You always have a choice," she said seriously. "Tomorrow I'm going into town."

"It looks like your mind's made up," Chase observed.

Jessie nodded. "Yup."

"And there's nothing I can say to dissuade you."

"Nope."

"All right. Then first thing in the morning we'll break camp and start off."

Jessie shook her head. "Not us, Chase. Just me."

"Now hold on, Jessie. If you're going into town I'm going with you."

"No."

"Jessie!"

"Someone has to stay here in case Ki shows up."

"If we're going into town, we should run into him."

"Chase, all we know is that Ki left for Waterville. We don't know where he is now."

"It stands to reason—"

Jessie cut him off. "No it doesn't. You don't know Ki," she said with a smile. Then she elaborated, "Look, Chase, maybe Dobson left town and Ki is following him. Maybe Ki's following one of Dobson's men. We don't know what Ki is up to. But I aim to find out."

"Fair enough," he conceded.

"And you're going to sit tight here and wait," she concluded. Chase started to object. "Sit!" she said forcefully.

"Woof, woof," he barked sarcastically.

In spite of herself, Jessie laughed. "I don't mean to treat you like a dog, Chase. But you have to understand it's important to have someone remain here to take a message. It really is."

"You know better than I do, Jessie. I'm just a simple surveyor," he said, though he didn't sound convinced.

"You're not just anything, and you're far from simple, and these have been two wonderful days we've spent together. But yes, I do know better than you when it comes to things like this."

"All right, I'll stay," he finally agreed. "But I won't like it."

Though the Waterville Hotel was nothing to brag about, the rooms were clean and the beds soft. Jessie asked for little else. She brushed out her hair, washed her face, then went down to the dining room for dinner. On her way she got more than her share of looks.

Jessie was used to it. Part of it was just friendly curiosity; a strange face in a small town always caused interest. Then too, with Jessie's shimmering hair, shapely breasts, and long, slim legs, she would have been very surprised if she didn't attract a few lingering glances. Surprised and disappointed.

And she didn't need any other disappointments today. She had arrived in town in a poor mood. It had been a dry, dusty ride, made worse by the realization that she missed Chase. In the last few days she had grown accustomed to his companionship.

But more importantly she was hoping to find Ki. Despite what she told Chase—and it was the truth—she half expected to find Ki sitting on the hotel porch. Silly as it was, she was disappointed to find that he wasn't.

Her disappointment grew as she searched the town and found no sign of him or his horse. And though she wanted to, she refrained from making any direct inquiries. Until she had a better idea of what was going on, she didn't want to be too blunt with her questions. She didn't know what kind of pose Ki had adopted, but a link between herself and Ki could compromise his position. Besides, a beautiful woman asking after an Oriental stranger would raise more than a few eyebrows. And curiosity was what she wanted to avoid.

She had finished with her meal and was nursing a cup of coffee when she became aware of a husky man hovering over her table. "May I help you?" she asked.

"You can ask me to pull up a chair." The speaker had broad shoulders and a fat neck.

"I'm afraid I don't know you, sir," Jessie replied.

He let out a booming laugh. "That's a good one," he said loudly. He seemed to be talking for the benefit of the whole room. "She's 'fraid she don't know me," he announced. Then he lowered his voice somewhat. "Ma'am, there's more reason to be afraid once you knows me."

This type of loud, brash man annoyed Jessie greatly, but she kept her calm. "Perhaps afraid was a poor choice of words. What I feel for you is not fear," she said coldly.

The man flashed an ugly grin at her. "I knew you'd cotton to me."

"Contempt is more like it." The man continued to stand there. "Perhaps you don't get my meaning," Jessie continued.

"Maybe you don't get mine," he answered. "I don't give up easily."

"And I don't appreciate being ogled," Jessie snapped.

"Don't take no offense, ma'am. We don't get many strangers in these parts."

"I'm sure you don't," she said in a voice that was not so harsh. With his mention of strangers, Jessie had become rather interested.

He sensed her soften and sat down. "Name's Colligan. Thomas Colligan." He waited for her to introduce herself, but when she didn't he picked up where he left off. "Like I was sayin', we don't get many strangers, and we never get one as pretty as you."

"That explains your lack of manners. If you got more people visiting your town, you'd know how to treat strangers."

Colligan let out a dry chuckle. "I know how to treat strangers."

Jessie didn't like the tone of his voice. "How? By being rude and insolent?"

"It usually ain't me that's the rude one."

"I bet," Jessie said. "You look the type that likes to run strangers right out of town."

"I don't know about that," he answered with a smile.

"When was the last stranger you had here?"

"A few nights ago."

"And where is he now?" Jessie asked.

"Who knows? He was just some coolie."

Jessie's interest sparked. Ki was often confused for Chinese. "And I suppose you ran him out of town because he was Chinese."

"Didn't have to run him out, ma'am. He left of his own accord. Though you might say I helped him out some. Even taught him some manners along the way."

"How's that?" Jessie wondered.

Colligan held up a meaty fist. "Decked him with one punch," he said proudly.

Inside Jessie flinched.

"He was bein' rude to me, ma'am," Colligan continued with an ugly grin.

Jessie found it hard to believe that this uncouth slug of a man could beat Ki in a fight. Perhaps it really was a full-blooded Chinaman. She had to get a description from Colligan. "I suppose it was quite difficult to knock out some small, roly-poly Chinese gentleman."

Colligan took the bait. "Hah, this fellow was as tall as me," he boasted, "and far from being fat."

"What's the difference how tall," Jessie teased, "if he's old and bald?"

He shook his head. "Long, black hair, and, oh, somewhere near my age, I reckon."

Jessie stood up. The description was too close to Ki's. "I have to be going . . ." she began.

"Hold it, missy," Colligan said gruffly. "We was just gettin' to know one another."

"I already know you well enough to know that I don't like you. Good day."

"Nobody walks away from me, missy," he said as he reached out and grabbed her arm. "You'll leave when I say."

"Let go of my arm."

Colligan laughed.

"I won't ask again!" Jessie snarled.

"Missy, before this night's over I'll be holdin' a lot more'n yer arm."

Without further ado Jessie slapped his face. Her hand made a sharp crack as it landed square on his cheek.

Colligan jumped to his feet, his chair falling over backwards as he did so.

He started to raise his fist. "You little tramp—" he began, but his words quickly disintegrated into a loud howl as Jessie's boot dug into his groin.

The moment his body had cleared the table, Jessie had seen her opportunity, and she took it. Now Colligan was doubled over, his face red and ugly as it screwed up in pain.

"A good kick goes a long way towards teaching someone like you proper manners," Jessie said calmly, and left the dining room.

A half-hour later Jessie was pulled from her thoughts by a knock on her door. Just enough time had passed, she realized, for Colligan to ply himself with enough whiskey to inflame his rage and build up his courage.

"This time, Mr. Colligan, it won't be my boot, but a .38 slug," she warned. "If you're standing there when I open this door you'll never have children. Are you sure you want me to open up?"

She heard a chuckle on the other side of the door. "Ma'am, it's Sheriff Johnson," the voice announced. "I just came to see if you were all right."

"Excuse my manners, sheriff," Jessie said as she opened the door.

The sheriff, a tal!, thin man in his early forties, was still smiling as he removed his hat. "No need to apologize. In fact that's what I came here to do."

"For what?" she asked.

125

"We try and run a civil town here, ma'am," he said apologetically. "But there's always going to be one bad apple in the bunch."

Jessie smiled. "No harm done."

"I wouldn't exactly say that," he said with a smile. "A well aimed boot can cause a heck of a lot of harm."

"And I aimed well?" Jessie asked innocently.

The sheriff nodded. "If you'd like to bring charges against the man . . . ?"

Jessie shook her head. "I think he's learned his lesson. But thank you for your concern, sheriff."

The man nodded. "I don't think he'll cause you any more trouble."

"In any event, I can take care of myself."

"I don't doubt it," he said with a smile and started to leave.

Jessie stopped him. "But, sheriff, there are those who can't. Colligan boasted about punching out an Oriental man the other night. What happened to him?"

"The Chinese?"

Jessie nodded.

The sheriff seemed unconcerned. "Left town, I reckon. If he would have come in and pressed charges we could have done something, but just lighting out like he done . . ." He ended with a shrug.

"I understand, sheriff. Good night."

As the door closed, a sense of foreboding overcame Jessie. Ki had been in town but had left. No one knew where he had gone; he had not been back to the camp. To Jessie's mind that meant only one thing—trouble.

It didn't take long for Jessie to figure out who might be the one responsible. Ki had come looking for answers. Perhaps he had found them, and then some.

The next morning, bright and early, Jessie was in the

saddle, heading straight for the Dobson house. What she would do when she got there remained to be seen, but she had no doubts that she was heading to the right place. If Ki wasn't there she would find out where he was.

When she dismounted in the front yard she had only a rough plan of action. She had decided there were to be no pleasantries and no beating around the bush. She would find out what happened to Ki—or else.

Ki carried a sack of potatoes up from the root cellar and dropped them in the kitchen.

"Thank you, Ki," Juanita said. "Now if you'll be so kind to serve this to *señor* Dobson. He's in the study." She indicated a tray with a pot of coffee and servings for two.

Ki carried the tray to the study, where he knocked softly, waited for a reply, then entered.

He was not an easy man to surprise, but for a brief moment he was so taken aback he almost walked into the back of a chair. He recovered before spilling any coffee, and when he placed the tray on the desk his face was once again calm and expressionless.

Ki poured the first cup of coffee and offered it to Dobson's guest.

Jessie was not so quick to recover, and still had her mouth open as she took the cup from Ki.

Dobson noticed her change of expression. "Is there anything wrong, Miss Starbuck?"

Jessie shook her head. "Nothing."

Dobson still looked concerned. "For a moment there you looked like you saw a ghost."

"I was just remembering something that I forgot to take care of."

Dobson nodded knowingly. "When you're running a large financial combine it's hard to take care of every last detail. I know. I can have my man run into town and send a wire off for you."

"It can wait," she answered with a smile. "But thank you."

Ki handed Dobson his cup.

"That will be all," the man said.

Ki nodded, and with a lingering look at Jessie, left.

Jessie could tell that Ki was mad at her. But that didn't matter. What did matter was that Ki was safe.

"Now as you were saying, Miss Starbuck. About your man you sent up here?"

Jessie was pulled from her thoughts. "Oh, yes, well, maybe it's no longer important," she muttered. After introducing herself, Jessie mentioned that she had sent a man up to Waterville to contact Dobson. She didn't say yet who or why. But now that she knew where Ki was, she no longer had to waste time with that problem. She had the freedom to pursue another course. She decided then to go directly for the bull's-eye, and try to find out about the land swindle.

She composed herself quickly. "My man might have been delayed along the way," she began. "And I made better time than I expected. To be honest, I much prefer dealing with you directly."

"Then what can I do for you?" Delbert said with a smile.

"I'm looking to buy land, grazing land."

"I see. And you wish to attract financiers, backers . . . ?"

"Of course not. It'll be part of the Circle Star. There are no partners or shareholders in my spread. I own it all," she said simply.

"Forgive me," he said humbly. "Then why come to me?"

128

"I'm interested in buying land around here."

"And you think I have land to sell?"

"Do you?" she asked bluntly.

"There is always land to sell, Jessie, but I don't know if I have enough to make it worth your while. I imagine a good-sized ranch requires a lot of land."

"I'll only be running about fifteen thousand head."

"You'll have to forgive me. I know very little about cattle."

"What I'm looking for, Mr. Dobson, is a range where I can fatten up my cattle after driving them north."

"From Texas?"

Jessie nodded. "Some of the herd would come from Texas."

"And why drive them all the way up here?" he asked. "Why not Kansas City?"

"The northern Pacific is going to be a big market," was her answer.

Dobson looked at her shrewdly. "But why buy land here? Why not ship them direct?"

Jessie could tell it was a leading question. She took her time with her answer. "Cattle will lose weight on a drive. Same in shipping. The longer they're away from good grazing the more weight they'll lose. And every pound is money."

"I see. But why choose Waterville?"

"It doesn't have to be Waterville *per se*," she explained. "Any area within a few days from here will be fine. I'll even go as far as Greenville."

Dobson shifted in his chair. Jessie could tell he was eyeing her suspiciously. "But I still don't understand why you chose this area, when if you went direct—"

"In time I plan to do just that," she interrupted him.

From the look on Dobson's face Jessie wasn't sure if he understood. "One day the railroad will run right through this region."

"What do you know about the railroad?" he demanded.

"What is there to know?" she said with a disarming smile. A few of the pieces began to fall in place. She suspected that the Dobson Deed and Trust Company, preparing for the coming of the railroad, was acquiring as much land as possible. That they didn't always do it legally probably did not concern them. It would, though, set Dobson on his guard when someone came poking around, as Jessie was doing now. She had to put him at ease. "You seem surprised, Mr. Dobson."

"No, not really."

"I'm somewhat familiar with the workings of railroads," she explained. "My father was a partner of Commodore Whiting's . . ."

"The Oregon Central?"

"The same," Jessie said with a nod.

"I see," he said seriously. Then he broke into a grin. "I gather an astute financier does have his, or in this case her, finger in many pies. It really is no secret that the railroad will eventually branch out, is it?"

Jessie shook her head. "The pattern of progress is easy to read."

Dobson smiled. "For some."

"The ability to see the changes coming is a necessary tool for survival," Jessie said simply.

Dobson leaned back in his chair. "I knew of your father, and though I never had the pleasure of meeting him I don't doubt you take after him."

"In many ways," Jessie agreed.

"But why do you suppose I have land to sell?"

Jessie realized this was the second of the delicate questions, but she didn't hesitate with her answer. "As a representative of the Dobson Company. . . ."

"Yes?"

"I thought you might have contacts with Eastern land speculators."

He leaned forward in his chair. "And why do you think that?"

"Remember, I'm am astute financier. I see the changes coming."

Dobson laughed, but was not totally accepting of her answer. "I believe you are, Miss Starbuck, but that still doesn't add up. . . ."

"Then why is Delbert Dobson living in Montana, and who is buying up the open range?" Her last words seemed to trouble Dobson, and Jessie feared she tipped her hand a bit too far. "You forget I'm a rancher first and foremost," she said with a smile. "I've already made certain inquiries," she said simply. "I always keep tabs on what's happening to good range land. It's my lifeblood."

Delbert seemed assuaged. "Of course," he said with a warm smile, but he didn't commit himself any further.

It was up to Jessie to forge ahead. "I imagine there must be some speculators that would be willing to sell now at a nice profit."

"I don't have to mention that when the rails come through here profits will rise steeply."

Jessie smiled. "Though I believe it, and you believe it, there are others, especially back East, who feel that that might be a big when. A nice profit today is often worth more than the promise of a killing sometime down the road."

"A bird in hand is worth two in the bush," Dobson said with a smile.

"Exactly."

"Miss Starbuck, you do your family name justice."

★

Chapter 12

At the dinner table Jessie sat to the left of Dobson, and directly across from Sylvia. As Ki served the meal he couldn't help notice that Jessie and Dobson were on a first-name basis. He also noticed the animosity with which Sylvia watched Jessie.

Things were shaping up interestingly, Ki thought to himself. All the players were in their places waiting for the action to start. But he was beginning to worry that maybe this wasn't the safest place for Jessie to be. He was just wondering how to convince her of this when the door to the kitchen opened and Jessie walked in.

"Oh excuse me," she said sweetly. "I must have taken a wrong turn."

"I'll show you to the study, ma'am," Ki offered politely, as he ushered her out to the hall.

The minute the kitchen door closed, Jessie leaned close to Ki. "Don't be mad, I can explain," she whispered quickly.

"There's no need to explain," Ki said. "I can figure it out."

"Oh?"

"You were tired of waiting around doing nothing. Am I right?"

Jessie looked hurt. "I was also worried about you, Ki. I thought something might have happened to you."

Ki stared at her.

Jessie stared back. "A dumb thought; I must have lost my head."

"We shouldn't be seen together," was Ki's response.

"We have to talk."

"I'll find a way," Ki assured her.

"Delbert asked me to stay over," she said carefully. "And I accepted." She watched Ki for his reaction.

"Tonight, then," he said hurriedly. "Behind the barn."

She nodded and returned to Dobson in the study.

The moon was full, and hung in a cloud-covered sky. For the most part it hid behind the clouds, but there were moments when it would peak through and light the night. Jessie waited in the shadow of the barn. Periodically she would hear a sound and turn, expecting to see Ki. But each time it was the wind, a mouse, or the creaking of the hayloft. Jessie waited patiently knowing that Ki would show up soon.

Even though she was expecting him, she was still startled by his soundless entrance. She sensed his presence more than heard it. She turned quickly around, and was face to face with him.

"Somehow I just knew you'd do that," she said softly.

"Good," he answered. "And do you know what I'm going to say?"

She shook her head.

"I'll give you a clue, Jessie. You're not going to like it."

"If you were going to tell me to go back, the answer is no. Dobson accepts me as an equal. I suspect he thinks we are of like minds. If I play my cards right it's possible he might let me in on the swindle." She spoke quickly, without pause. She stopped to take a breath, then continued. "Now what was it you were going to say?" she said with a sweet smile.

"Must have slipped my mind," Ki answered.

"I thought so."

"But Jessie, you realize that if he suspects you're trying to set him up . . ."

"That's why I'm glad you're here. It will—"

"Quiet!" Ki commanded.

Jessie didn't ask why; she stopped talking immediately. In the silence she thought she heard something, but wasn't sure. Then a moment later she heard what she thought was a muffled footstep. They weren't alone.

Ki leaned over and whispered in her ear, "Lie face down and don't move till I get back."

Jessie did as he asked. She understood that in a prone position not only would she appear to be a log, but lying down, the white skin of her face wouldn't reflect the moonlight.

She didn't hear Ki move away, and she wouldn't hear him come back. But she knew that when he did the problem would be taken care of.

Ki moved soundlessly to the front of the barn. Even though his eyes were accustomed to the dark he couldn't see anybody. He took two steps inside the barn and listened. After a moment it came to him—the sound of breathing. It was one man and he was standing not far from Ki.

The fact that the intruder was not moving led Ki to

believe that the man was also listening. That made it much more difficult.

Ki wondered what had brought the man to the barn. Had he heard Jessie leave the house? Had he overheard any of their conversation? Or was it something else entirely that brought him out here? At the present moment the whys and wherefores mattered little. What was important was that the man was on his guard, waiting, listening.

Ki bent down and picked up a small stone. He moved with such fluidity his clothes did not even rustle. The man was somewhere on his right. He tossed the stone across to the left. It landed with a soft thud, but in the silence of the barn it rang out like a shot.

Ki could hear the man's breath stop. Then he heard movement. As Ki had hoped, the man was moving towards him.

He readied himself. He knew he would only have one chance. He had no doubt the man carried a gun. If Ki didn't bring the man down with the first blow, the intruder would get a shot off. Ki wasn't worried about the gun as a weapon; the man would be shooting in the dark. But even a single wild shot could mean disaster.

It would wake the house and send men running to the barn. Ki would be hard pressed to explain what he and Jessie were doing outside together. It was far better to make sure the man never got the chance to fire a shot.

Ordinarily that would not present much of a problem. There were numerous *atemi* points throughout the body that could render a man unconscious. The trick was to find the pressure points in the dark.

Suddenly the movements stopped. The man was listening. Ki held his breath. He doubted the man was more than a yard away.

"My men have the barn surrounded," the man said in a

normal tone, but in the deathly quiet it sounded like a shout.

Ki was surprised the man spoke; it gave away his position. If Ki had a gun and was so inclined, he would have a very good chance at hitting the mark.

The man continued, "You can't escape. Throw down your gun and give yourself up."

Ki smiled. He could hear the doubt in the man's voice. That, combined with the lie about the barn being surrounded, led Ki to suspect the man was having second thoughts. Perhaps the man was thinking to himself that he had only imagined a sound. Maybe there really was no one else in the barn. Ki could almost feel the man relax his guard. Maybe he even took his finger off the trigger of his gun.

The man took a step.

The time to strike was now.

Ki shot out his fist. There was no problem directing the blow. The man was so close Ki could hear the breath escape his mouth. At this range he decided not to bother with the *atemi* points. A solid fist, he reasoned, would work just as well. Ki aimed straight for the face, striking with the force of a sledgehammer.

There was a surprised grunt, a dull thud, then nothing.

Ki didn't linger. He went right out to Jessie. "Let's go back to the house," he said quietly.

"Who was it?" she asked as she got up.

"I don't know. I didn't look."

"What?" Jessie said with surprise.

"I didn't want to light a match," he answered.

"But Ki, it might be important to know."

He smiled. "We'll know. Tomorrow." Jessie started to say something and Ki cut her off. "Believe me, Jessie, come tomorrow it will be no secret."

"One other thing, Ki . . ."

"Yes."

"I'm going to stick around till I get to the bottom of this."

Ki did not protest.

"What, no argument?" Jessie chided.

"At the first sign of trouble, you're on your horse and out of here." There was solid conviction behind his words. He knew better than to argue with Jessie, but at the same time he would never allow Jessie to remain in a situation that threatened her safety.

For her part Jessie knew not to argue with Ki, either. She also understood.

They said good night, then silently returned to their rooms.

The next morning, even before breakfast, they did indeed find out what happened in the barn.

Hank, the stable boy, had been the one that found the foreman. The man was lying unconscious in the barn. A bucket of water quickly revived him, and he was soon able to tell what had happened.

The foreman said he had come out of the bunkhouse for a smoke and thought he heard some noise over at the barn. They had been having trouble with horse thieves, and the foreman thought he might be catching them in the act. He entered the barn and was knocked out by what he guessed must have been a fence pole. His efforts, though, were not in vain. He did manage to scare off the rustlers; come morning all the horses were still in their stalls.

Dobson sent Juanita to tend to the foreman. She had experience dealing with the sick and wounded. She returned shortly, announcing that although it was an ugly-

138

looking bruise, there was no serious damage—nothing that a day or two of rest wouldn't cure.

That worry aside, it was time to serve breakfast. Afterwards, Dobson told Ki to go into town and meet the late-morning stage; he was expecting a business associate to arrive.

Ki hitched up the buggy and started on his way. He was a little apprehensive about leaving Jessie, but he convinced himself nothing bad would happen.

In fact, much to his chagrin, very little was happening. The foreman's story answered one of Ki's questions—why the foreman was wearing a gun around the yard. It was not unknown for brazen horse thieves to strike in the middle of the day. Now that he knew the foreman had a reason for carrying a weapon, Ki no longer viewed him as a hired gun. That narrowed down Ki's list of suspects. With a dry smile he realized he was glad that Jessie had worked her way into Dobson's confidence. Maybe she could succeed where he had failed.

Dobson looked across the desk to Jessie. "I guess I don't have to tell you there are great things in store for this land."

"Not unless you have something particular in mind."

Dobson smiled. "I do and I don't. I can't tell you just yet, Jessie. But believe me, I want you to be a part of it."

"If I knew more about it, maybe I could be."

"There are far too many shortsighted people in this world, Jessie. They look at something and can't see the possibilities." He stood up and went to look out the window. "They see a hill, and they see trees and grass. Maybe a few realize it's a good place for a farm or a ranch, but that's all."

"To many folks, that's all there is," Jessie said sensitively. "A home of their own, some land—that's all they want out of life."

Dobson turned to face her. "And that's all they'll get."

"There's nothing wrong with that," Jessie insisted.

Dobson moved close to her. "Of course there isn't." His voice was soft, but there was no tenderness to his words. "They're the backbone of this country. But we, Jessie, we are the cream."

"Sometimes the cream has austere beginnings," Jessie reminded him. "Frémont started as a second lieutenant. Charlie Goodnight started with a modest ranch. James Hill started as a stock boy."

"But Jessie, not every stock boy grows up to own railroads," he said, sitting down next to her on the settee.

"No, of course not," she agreed. "But can you say which one will and which one won't?"

"I'm not trying to," he answered simply. "All I'm saying is that people don't realize the wealth of opportunity that lies out there. They don't realize what's lying just around the bend."

"Maybe not," she said simply. She had a feeling Dobson had something very specific in mind, and she wanted to keep nudging him till she knew what it was. "Sometimes there are surprises waiting that no one expected. We can't predict the future."

"No, but we can plan for it," he answered excitedly.

"A man could get very rich doing that," she said leadingly. She held her breath awaiting his response.

Delbert nodded. "But there is something even better than riches, Jessie. Power."

Just then the door opened.

"Oh, excuse me, Father, I didn't mean to disturb you," Sylvia stammered.

Dobson rose quickly. "That's all right, daughter." She

turned to leave and he stopped her. "Sylvia, this afternoon I'll be busy with Mr. Williams. If you're going riding later, I'd like you to take Jessie along with you."

"That's considerate of you, Delbert, but there's really no need to bother your daughter," Jessie said quickly.

Delbert didn't answer. He turned to Sylvia, letting her decide.

"It's no bother, Father. I'd be happy to entertain Miss Starbuck." She smiled as she spoke, but there was a coldness to her words. She then turned and stared directly at Jessie, as if she were offering a challenge.

"That's rather nice of you," Jessie said, as she stared back at her. The challenge was accepted.

Dobson had no idea of the animosity that was developing between these two women. "Good. Now perhaps it's best if I get to work. There are a few papers I have to prepare for Mr. Williams."

"I understand," Jessie said, as she stood up and headed out the door.

"Have a pleasant ride," he told them both.

"Don't worry father, we will."

When the stagecoach pulled into town and unloaded its passengers, there was no question who Dobson's associate was. He was the first man off, a heavyset individual in his early fifties. He wore a bowler hat, a long black jacket, and a silk vest with a very conspicuous gold watch-fob. And if that weren't enough, the parts of his face that were not covered by his large mutton chops were pale and pasty. Ki laughed to himself; the perfect Yankee dude.

Ki went over and introduced himself. Then, taking the valise, he escorted Mr. Williams to the buggy.

On the way home, Ki began to get a very odd feeling about the man that sat behind him. He wondered what his business was, and if he had anything to do with the land swindle. Somehow Ki meant to find out.

It turned out to be easier than he thought. After Mr. Williams had a bath, a change of clothes, and a hot cup of coffee, he and his host went for a buggy ride—with Ki sitting right up front in the driver's seat.

★

Chapter 13

For the first few miles, nothing of any interest was discussed. Dobson and Williams exchanged pleasantries, talked about mutual friends, and commented on the weather.

Ki heard a sharp slap and a soft cuss. He guessed that Williams had just been bitten by a mosquito. Williams' next comment proved him right. "Damn bugs," the man said with annoyance. "Damned country," he added a moment later. "Why bother with this god forsaken piece of..."

"Don't go blaming the territory," Dobson said with a laugh. "There are bugs in Washington, too."

"There you are not forced to conduct business in the wilds. I've never once been bitten at the club," Williams said indignantly.

"I gather they still don't allow pests past the front door," Dobson remarked, tongue in cheek.

"Make fun if you wish, Delbert, but there's much to be said for the civilized life."

Again Dobson laughed. "We're not barbarians out here, Thomas."

"You just live like them."

"To be honest, I don't miss Baltimore at all," Dobson said sincerely. Williams didn't answer, and Dobson continued. "There are perhaps a few sacrifices that must be made, but all in all I think this land gives more than it takes."

"I'm not convinced," Williams said dryly.

"Then look around."

"At what? There's nothing but trees."

"I happen to like trees," Dobson said with a touch of humor.

"Good for you, Delbert."

"Thomas, you've a small mind. You don't realize you're looking at a veritable kingdom. A man can build a fortune, and rule like a king."

There was a spirit in Dobson that Ki couldn't help but admire. However, he didn't respect the possibility that Dobson was trying to build his empire by devious means. Cheating honest men out of their land could never be justified.

"May I remind you that that was the initial plan," Williams said. "And I'm happy to report that I think the climate is turning favorable," he added proudly. "Events may start moving faster than we expected."

Ki couldn't see, but he suspected that Dobson had silenced his associate with a hand gesture; the conversation ended abruptly.

"Ki, follow that trail to the right," Dobson instructed. Then turning back to Williams, he continued: "It leads to the lake. It's a nice walk along the bank."

Williams understood. So did Ki. In effect Dobson was saying, "Shut up, we'll talk when we're alone."

Ki pulled the buggy to a stop in a small meadow just a few yards from the shore of the lake. The two men stepped out.

"Wait here for us," Dobson told Ki. "We won't be long."

Ki did as he was told, at least until the two men were out of sight. He had no intention of letting them discuss matters in private. He had every intention of eavesdropping. He had a feeling, a strong feeling, that their discussion would be about irregular, if not downright illegal, activities. Perhaps it would even explain the swindle the Dobson Deed and Trust Company was trying to pull off.

Ki strolled casually down to the water's edge. If he happened to be noticed, he hoped it would appear as if he were only stretching his legs. But Dobson did not spot him; the two men were already about thirty yards off to Ki's right.

At this part of the lake the water came right up to the grassy shore. There was no way Ki could get close enough to overhear their conversation. There was no way he could even follow them without being spotted. He quickly scanned the lake. About a hundred and fifty yards ahead, the bank rose steeply into a grove of thick pine trees. If Dobson continued that far he would pass right through the grove; there was no way to avoid it.

Ki raced back to the buggy. Then, staying out of sight, he ran a wide circle to the pine grove. He easily beat the two men to the trees. He selected a large pine in the middle of the stand, and was soon safely tucked out of sight in the notch of a high bough. From this position he would be able to hear anything that was said below. Dobson and Williams had only to venture this far.

He was in luck. A minute later, the two men came into

sight. Williams was breathing hard, obviously out of breath from the simple climb. "Good lord, Delbert, what are you trying to do to me?" he gasped.

"You've gotten fat and lazy sitting around the club," Dobson answered teasingly. "You should move out here and spend a few months."

Williams leaned against a tree. "I'd die first."

Dobson laughed. "You might die out here. But chances are we'd make a real man out of you yet."

"I don't wish to be made into anything. I'm quite happy the way I am, thank you."

Dobson lowered himself to the ground. He chuckled when he saw his companion's shocked expression. "Sit down, Thomas."

"But . . ."

"Juanita can clean your clothes when we get back. Now sit."

After the initial shock of sitting on the ground, Williams seemed happy to be off his feet.

"Now how are the negotiations progressing?" Dobson asked.

"Good," Williams said with a smile. "Finally the railroad has agreed to carry homesteaders free of charge."

"I had no doubt they would."

"You were right," Williams conceded. "Though I don't know how you could have been so positive."

"Simple business, Thomas."

"It doesn't seem like good business to ship passengers for nothing."

Delbert laughed. "Thomas, it's amazing how uninventive you can be."

"I fail to see what inventiveness has to do with running a profitable railroad," Williams said, somewhat insulted.

"As you were so quick to point out earlier, there's not much out here but trees."

"I remember making that observation."

"Trees don't need the services of a railroad."

"No, of course not," Williams said, slightly annoyed.

"But homesteaders do," Dobson said flatly. "Once this land gets settled, the railroads will be needed to ship goods, supplies, and people. By bringing in the first wave of settlers free of charge, the railroad is in effect creating a market where there once was nothing. Only trees," he added with a laugh.

Williams nodded, then moved quickly on to the next point. "And Senator Fredricks has been pushing hard for another census. He's been arguing, rather effectively, that Montana has as much a right to be admitted into the union as does Colorado."

"Colorado's been a state since '76."

"That's Fredrick's point. He says it's high time we corrected this oversight."

"And what of the opposition?" Dobson asked.

"There's enough money coming out of Helena that the opposition is dwindling."

"And the territorial governor?"

"He knows his position is strong only as long as Hayes stays in office."

"Which won't be long," Dobson said happily.

"Now," Williams began with a smile, "if we were in the club, instead of out here, I'd lift my glass to the first governor of the state of Montana."

"There'll be plenty of time for that later. Anything else?"

Williams shook his head.

"Then let's start back, unless of course you'd like to continue around the lake?"

147

"The governor has quite a sense of humor," Williams said as he pulled himself to his feet.

"There are some beaver dams along the north shore."

"Please, Delbert."

Dobson laughed. "Thomas, have you ever seen a beaver?"

"Nor do I care to," Williams said in all seriousness.

"Where's your natural wonder, your curiosity? Will anything make you happy?"

"Yes. A soft chair and a cool drink."

"You're an easy man to satisfy," Dobson said as he led the way back.

Ki waited a moment, then softly dropped to the ground. At an easy run he set off through the trees. There was no real rush; he knew he would make it back before the two men.

A few minutes later, he was leaning against the buggy, watching Dobson and Williams make their way up from the lake.

Sylvia's mount was a coal-black Arabian stallion. It was a fine animal, strong and well-groomed, the like of which was rare on the frontier. An animal like that cost more than many a small rancher's entire stock. The value of the horse did not escape Sylvia. She rode it proudly, happily flaunting her expensive possession.

Sylvia was an experienced rider; Jessie could tell from the way she sat in the saddle. She rode with squared shoulders and a straight back. She also moved easily with the horse. Jessie also noted that Sylvia rode an English saddle.

Though there was nothing wrong with that, Jessie had a natural dislike for those saddles—or more specifically, the people who chose to ride them. In England, where the terrain was, at worst, rolling hills, a shallow seat had few drawbacks. But in the rugged land of the American West, a deep bowl was a necessity. And in extremely steep and rocky areas a double-fire saddle was a common choice. Also known as a Texas rig, this saddle had two cinches and an even deeper seat. In mountainous regions, riding a horse with an English saddle was either a sign of stupidity or ignorance.

But Jessie didn't think Sylvia was guilty of either. Sylvia rode English to be different, to prove she was better. Most folk learned to ride the way they learned to walk—in time you just did it. But English riders were always trained. Jessie was familiar with the way rich Easterners learned about horsemanship—riding academies, instructors, private lessons. There was something silly to it all. And it was exemplified best by the special duds they wore when riding. Sylvia wore them all; the felt-covered black cap, the baggy pants, and the high-legged, gloss-finished riding boots.

The horse, the clothes, the saddle, all drew attention to Sylvia. They pointed out that she was better than the rest.

Then Jessie realized what she disliked most about an English saddle. In the West a horse was everything. It was more than a means of transportation; it was a man's livelihood. And the saddle was designed with that in mind. Despite what Eastern tenderfoots thought, a saddlehorn was not to hang on to. It was utilitarian. It was made to fasten a rope to. Jessie couldn't imagine roping cattle without a saddlehorn. Likewise the shape of the seat—it was designed to allow a man to ride comfortably for many hours. The Western saddle also made it possible to tie down various bundles and supplies. A bedroll, rifle, canteen, and a few days' food were an easy addition to any cowboy's saddle. Try doing that on an English saddle, Jessie thought to herself. The Western saddle was all business. It was not meant for leisure riding or sport. It was a working man's tool.

On the other hand, an English saddle announced to the world that its rider had no need to earn a living on horseback, that he would never have to travel long days in the saddle. It effectively said, "I am better than you."

Jessie looked at Sylvia. The woman was rich, haughty, and conceited. She would never have to work a day in her life. Any long trip would be taken by stage, wagon or railroad. She didn't need an English saddle to prove that to anyone. It was excessive and arrogant, just like Sylvia. Jessie almost had to laugh; for all that Sylvia thought of herself, she was anything but better.

Jessie was pulled from her thoughts by Sylvia's voice. "I usually run Sultan quite a bit. He can fly like the wind."

"He's a fine horse," Jessie agreed.

Sylvia smiled. "If I go too fast for you, just let me know," she said sweetly.

"I'll try and keep up," Jessie answered. She didn't think she'd have any trouble. There were few riders, male or female, that could handle a horse as well as Jessie could. But she didn't bother to mention that.

Sylvia used her riding crop, and the stallion burst into a fast gallop. Jessie, more gentle with her mount, followed close behind. A mile later, Sylvia slowed her horse and turned to look for Jessie. Disappointment was written all over her face when she realized Jessie was not far behind.

The riding crop smacked against the stallion's rump, and they were off on another run.

They passed the early afternoon in this game of equestrian-follow-the-leader. Sylvia led the way, and tried every possible maneuver to show up Jessie. But when Sylvia jumped over a fallen tree trunk and Jessie followed right behind, Sylvia, at least to herself, admitted she could not best her companion.

"You're quite a rider," Sylvia said grudgingly. "You surprise me."

"I've been riding my whole life," Jessie explained.

"Too bad it won't do you any good."

"I don't understand," Jessie said honestly.

"My father doesn't ride."

"That's odd," Jessie remarked.

"He prefers the buggy."

"But I don't see what that has to do with—"

Sylvia didn't let her finish. "You won't be able to impress my father with your riding, the way you've been impressing him with that smile of yours."

"Sylvia, this is no concern of yours," Jessie began, "but I came here on business. My dealings with your father have been strictly business."

"I see the way you look at him," Sylvia said with contempt.

Jessie was patient. She refused to lose her temper, and remained firm. "Your father is interesting, good-looking, and polite, but it may disappoint you to know that I have no designs on him."

"You're a liar," Sylvia snapped.

"You may find I am many things, but a liar is not one of them," Jessie said calmly.

Sylvia looked her in the eye. "Perhaps I am wrong. Perhaps I owe you an apology." She smiled sweetly.

Jessie was not fooled. "I think you do," she said simply.

Quite knowingly, Sylvia changed the subject. "There's a stream just past those trees. We'll stop there for lunch." Without waiting for a response she started her horse in that direction.

They ate in relative silence, exchanging only a few curt words. When Sylvia finished her meal, she stood up and went to her horse. Without even a look to see if Jessie was ready to ride, she swung up into the saddle.

Jessie would have been happy to let her go on by herself, but she could foresee the problems that would cause. Sylvia would have to explain why Jessie had been left to return alone, and in all likelihood her answer would include her hypotheses on the relationship between her father and Jessie. And that might provoke Dobson into asking Jessie a few questions. Delbert did seem rather sweet on her, and Jessie preferred to avoid discussing the topic altogether. With a sigh, she went to her own horse. It was easier to ride with the brat than to have to face Delbert's questions. Jessie could put up with Sylvia a little longer.

Jessie was tightening the cinch when her horse suddenly shied away. Instinct alone caused her to turn; it saved her life.

Sylvia's stallion was rearing up on its hind legs. Its front legs came crashing down just inches from where Jessie stood.

She scrambled quickly out of the way, but the stallion acted like an animal possessed. It continued to buck and kick.

For a brief moment, Jessie was concerned about Sylvia. The woman could be seriously hurt if she were thrown from the saddle. Even if she escaped injury in the fall, there was the very real danger of being trampled by the horse's hooves. Jessie dodged the horse, yet stayed as close as possible so that in the event Sylvia did fall, Jessie would be there to drag her to safety.

Then Jessie got a good look at Sylvia, and froze in anger. She expected to see a scared, helpless woman. Instead, she saw a calm, controlled rider with a face stretched into a cold, calculating grin.

The stallion reared up again, and Jessie backed off quickly. But she tripped and went sprawling on her back. She instantly knew the danger she was in. She had seen enough men trampled by a bucking bronc. She knew what she had to do. She also knew she had to act immediately.

The crucial mistake was to delay. Often a downed rider waited to see which way a wild horse was moving before he tried to get out of the way. That was usually a fatal mistake. Once an animal reared down on you, it was unlikely you could get away in time. The trick was to move immediately. It didn't matter which direction. If you acted quickly enough, you could usually get out beyond the range of the horse.

Jessie rolled quickly to her right. She didn't stop until she had completed a half-dozen turns. It was hard work, but it was easier than getting trampled to death.

When she thought she had outdistanced the horse, she sprang quickly to her feet.

The stallion came charging at her. This time Jessie knew it wasn't a spooked horse, but a crazy rider. She had no doubt that Sylvia was trying to run her down.

Jessie knew it was pointless to try and outrun the stallion. There was only one other choice. She stood her ground till the last minute, then quickly stepped to the side. As the horse passed, Jessie jumped up and tried to grab hold of Sylvia. Her hand caught the woman's waist, but then lost its hold. Her hand slid down, but managed to catch a hold of Sylvia's boot. Jessie hung on tight.

There was a brief moment of stasis—a time of delicate balance. Jessie hung steadfastly to Sylvia's leg. Any second she would lose her grip and fall flat on her face. She waited expectantly. Her grip tightened. Then the equilibrium broke.

The rider came toppling down, landing hard.

Jessie grabbed Sylvia roughly and lifted her to her feet.

"I don't know what happened," Sylvia said in a panic. "I couldn't control him."

Jessie slapped her, twice. "Don't ever try that again," she hissed.

Sylvia, in tears, gasped, "Don't you ever lay a hand on me again."

"Or what?" Jessie challenged. She didn't take kindly to having been nearly trampled to death.

For her answer Sylvia lunged at Jessie. Her nails went directly for Jessie's face.

Jessie didn't retreat. She stepped to the side and landed a fist deep into the other woman's gut. It wasn't much of a punch, but it took Sylvia by surprise. She doubled over and gasped.

"Would you like to try that again?" Jessie taunted. Ki had taught her some martial arts, and though she was good at it, she wasn't good enough to defeat a strong man. Sylvia, though, was neither a man nor strong. Jessie stood ready.

Sylvia straightened, and seemed composed. "There's no need for that," she said calmly, as she walked towards Jessie. But as she got close she attacked again, this time grabbing for Jessie's hair.

Sylvia fought like a woman. That was her main problem. Jessie knew how to fight like a man. It was no contest.

One punch later, Sylvia was sitting on the ground, crying. Her face was in her hands, and Jessie could see the blood dripping out of her nose.

It would be a shame if her nose were broken, Jessie

thought to herself. But she knew there wasn't enough wallop in her punch. It was just a simple bloody nose.

Jessie went to her horse and swung into the saddle. The black stallion was grazing innocently a few yards away. He seemed impervious to all the commotion. Jessie went over to him, curious as to why the animal had gone seemingly loco. The answer was easy to come by.

On the horse's right flank was a series of tiny gashes. They could have been caused by a small blade, or more likely, a large hairpin. In either case they would have been responsible for the wild behavior of the stallion.

Jessie stroked the animal's soft nose, then grabbed hold of the bit. She led the horse to where Sylvia sat crying. "It's a shame to treat a fine animal this way," she said with disgust, and turned and started back to the house.

A few minutes later, Jessie came to an ironic realization. The English riding style that had been Sylvia's pride had also been the woman's undoing. The English saddle, with its shorter, smaller stirrups, couldn't hold Sylvia's leg in place. When Jessie grabbed hold of the leg it easily slid out. With a Western saddle, things would have turned out quite different. The deep stirrups would have held the leg firmly and Jessie would have wound up face down. She shivered at the thought, then smiled. Pride does go before a fall.

Chapter 14

After supper, Dobson and Williams lit up cigars, and Jessie excused herself to get a breath of fresh air. Ki noticed her absence and made an excuse to have to go out to the barn.

They met in the back, and told each other excitedly of their day.

"Governor!" Jessie exclaimed. "It's all starting to make sense."

Ki nodded. "If he can establish enough of his friends as landowners in the territory, not only can he swing statehood, but he can walk right in to the governor's chair."

"There's one thing, though, that I don't understand. Why bother running families off their land?"

"You're thinking of Josh Hainley?" Ki asked.

Jessie nodded. "Seems he could have fixed an election easily enough without even bothering with that."

"Maybe it's nothing more than simple greed," Ki suggested.

"Dobson doesn't strike me as an excessively greedy person."

Ki gave her a harsh look. "Can you be sure of that, Jessie?"

She remained firm. "Call it a hunch, but I don't think greed is the answer."

"No, of course not," Ki said suddenly. "It's not *more* land he needed, but *certain* land."

"What was so special about Hainley's Box H?" Jessie asked. "It was good grazing, but that doesn't make it unique."

"It's location did, though. Even with all of Dobson's influential friends he still needed the popular vote," Ki began.

"Don't misunderstand me, Ki, but that's easy enough to buy."

"Exactly. And it ties right in with the railroad. They bring out the settlers free of charge—"

"And we know why," Jessie added.

"Then the railroad supports Dobson for governor—"

"And the homesteaders, knowing where their best interests lie, elect Dobson."

"Exactly."

"But I still don't see why Dobson had to run Josh Hainley off."

"Because the railroad wanted that land. Or maybe because Dobson wanted them to have it. I can't be sure."

"I can understand the railroad wanting it," Jessie said. "Once they're up and running it would be in their interest to have the most cost-effective route."

Ki was silent a moment, then shook his head. "That's all true, but now that I think about it, Dobson probably wanted the railroad to have that land."

"What makes you say that, Ki?"

"Most of the land around the Box H was flat plain. It would make little difference where the railroad laid its tracks. Unless of course you wanted the railroad to come straight into Waterville."

The plot thickens, Jessie thought to herself. "With the exception of the mountains, it's almost a straight run from Greenville to Waterville," she noted aloud.

"And we know what a few hundred sticks of dynamite can do to a stubborn mountain," Ki said with a dry smile.

"It makes perfect sense now," Jessie said excitedly. "The way the railroad is laid will eventually determine the capital city. With the railroad going directly to Waterville, Helena will be knocked out of the running."

"And Waterville is Dobson's," Ki said flatly. Then he smiled. "You were right, Jessie, it's not greed we're talking about."

Jessie shook her head. She repeated Dobson's own words. "There are more important things than riches— there's power."

"They always seem to go hand in hand," Ki observed.

Suddenly a thought struck Jessie. "Ki, we know what the game is, but we still don't have any solid proof."

"We have the ledger," Ki reminded her.

"That's enough to take him into court," she agreed. "But I was hoping for something stronger—strong enough that a lengthy legal battle would be unnecessary."

"The one flaw in the scheme?"

Jessie nodded. "There has to be a weak link some-where," she said thoughtfully. "But we won't find it out here," she added with a smile.

Ki nodded, and they walked back to the house.

That was their one mistake.

From her bedroom window, Sylvia watched Jessie and Ki return to the house.

The next day Dobson prepared to go on a short business trip. "Mr. Williams and myself have to visit a few nearby ranches," he explained to Jessie. "I'll be gone for only a few days. You're welcome to stay."

"That's kind of you, but I wouldn't want to impose. The hotel will do just fine. . . ."

"Let me rephrase my request," he said with a smile. "I'd like you to stay here while I'm gone. I don't like leaving Sylvia alone."

Jessie looked like she was thinking it over, when all she was doing was playing hard to get. She wanted nothing more than a chance to snoop around without worrying about Delbert discovering her.

"I'd appreciate it if you stayed," Dobson repeated.

"If you'd like," Jessie finally agreed.

"Good."

They departed shortly thereafter. Ki went along to drive the buggy. But before he left, he had a moment alone with Jessie.

"Watch out for Sylvia," he warned.

Jessie smiled. "I don't think she'll give me any more trouble."

"I don't trust her," Ki said by way of a simple warning.

"I don't either, but I can handle her," Jessie said confidently.

"I imagine you can at that," Ki said with a smile. "You've handled much worse."

The buggy was barely out of sight when Jessie went to the barn and saddled her horse.

Her main purpose was to inform Chase as to her whereabouts. But she also realized there were a few things that needed looking into, and Chase could begin the investigation.

But after an hour of riding, her mind started wandering. She remembered how nice it was to have Chase hold her in his arms. The warm sun and the gentle motion of the horse lulled her into a peaceful state, and soon she was no longer confining her thoughts to a welcoming hug. She had developed an itch that only Chase could scratch. She urged her horse into a trot.

Chase had spent a restless night worrying about Jessie and Ki. He realized Ki could take care of himself; for that matter so could Jessie. Although, he told himself repeatedly, there was nothing to worry about, he did so just the same. He needed to be more patient. Eventually he drifted off to sleep, but only after promising himself that if no word came by nightfall of the next day, he would take a ride into town.

By morning his promise was forgotten. He'd be damned if he'd wait around like a tethered calf. He saddled his horse and was on the road to town before the sun had fully risen.

Sylvia was in such a hurry she didn't even notice that Jessie's horse was not in its stall. Perhaps if she had saddled her own horse she might have noticed. But she was in the barn for only the briefest minute; just long enough to tell Hank, the stable boy, that she wanted Sultan saddled and ready immediately. Impatiently, she waited outside, and heaven help that lazy boy if he dawdled needlessly.

He didn't. A few minutes later he came out leading the black stallion. "I'd be careful, Miss Sylvia, 'bout those

160

thornbushes. They can cause some mighty nasty scratches." He pointed to the animal's right flank.

"Mind your business," she snapped.

"Yes, ma'am," he said as he locked his hands together to give her a boost up into the saddle. "It's just those bushes can cut a man pretty bad, too. I wouldn't want you to fall in any."

Sylvia ignored him and, with a good slap, sent her horse flying out of the yard.

Hank turned back to the barn. "Like hell I wouldn't," he muttered to himself.

Jessie knew there was something wrong the minute she reined in at the camp. There was no bedroll, no horse, and no McReedy. She dismounted and studied the ground. She didn't see any signs of a fight, and there were no other bootmarks. The only fresh tracks were made by her horse and an animal whose print she recognized as belonging to Chase's horse.

She swung back into her saddle. More than likely, Chase had gotten tired of waiting and had gone into town to have a look around for himself. She couldn't blame him. She had done the same. She didn't wait for Ki either, she told herself.

She'd probably find McReedy in the saloon, beer in hand. A man could develop a powerful thirst doing nothing all day, day in, day out. Then there was the matter of food. Although McReedy did have enough food to last, there was the question of variety. A man could get pretty tired of salt pork, jerky, and beans.

Jessie smiled. After a beer, McReedy would probably head for a hot meal; perhaps a fresh beef stew. And why shouldn't he? Though McReedy couldn't have known, the main objection to his going to town no longer existed.

161

They hadn't wanted McReedy to be spotted by Dobson, but now that the man was out of town, there was nothing to worry about.

So why did Jessie feel apprehensive?

Sylvia rode into the livery, and the stable hand came running up. He offered her a hand down, then reached for the horse's reins.

"I'll take care of Sultan," she told him. Clearly he was surprised. If she noticed, Sylvia made no mention of it. She continued, "I'd like you to run an errand for me."

"Anything you'd like, ma'am."

Sylvia told him. He started off, and she called him back. "I'd like this be strictly between us," she reminded him.

"Of course, ma'am."

She handed him two silver dollars. "I think that's enough to ensure my privacy," she said with a haughty smile.

The stable hand didn't seem offended. He pocketed the money and ran off.

A few minutes later, Colligan swaggered into the stable. Sylvia was waiting.

"I need you," she began.

"Didn't think it'd be so soon," he said with a toothy grin. "The last time weren't more'n a week ago."

"Shut up!" she snapped. "I told you never to talk about that."

The grin faded from his face.

"It's a job. If necessary, I'll pay you for it."

"It ain't quite on the up and up?"

"Fool! If it was, would I come to you? I'd have one of my men do it."

He nodded. "How dirty is it?"

162

"That's entirely up to you," she answered.

"Okay, let's hear it."

"There's a woman staying at the house. She's a nuisance. I'd like her taken care of."

"I hear you."

"I don't care what you do, just so long as she doesn't come around bothering my father."

"You want her taken care of permanently?" he asked.

"I told you, I don't care. She's yours to do with as you please. Just so long as she doesn't come around the house."

Sylvia described the woman, and Colligan's face lit up. "It'll be a real pleasure," he announced triumphantly.

Chapter 15

Jessie tied her horse to the rail outside the Mad Dog. She started into the saloon, but didn't even go through the bat wings. From the door, she could see that Chase was not one of the few men who were standing at the bar.

She crossed the street and hurried to the restaurant, but again Chase was not there.

As a last resort she tried the hotel. She didn't really believe that Chase would have taken a room there, but he might have gone there to inquire about her own whereabouts. The hotel clerk, though, had no recollection of seeing a man that fit Chase's description.

Confused and a little worried, Jessie went to the livery. McReedy's horse was not there, and the stable hand didn't remember any stranger putting up his horse in the past few days. Jessie thanked him and rushed back to her horse.

Hoping to pick up some sign, she started to head back to the camp. She had barely gotten out of town when she realized that it was not only senseless—the road was too heavily traveled to distinguish Chase's tracks—but also pointless.

If McReedy left the camp, he must have done so for a reason. And if that reason wasn't a beer or a decent meal . . . Suddenly, it became obvious why McReedy had left, and where he was going.

She turned her horse around and headed straight for the Dobson house.

McReedy had come to town looking for her. Whether he found out that she was staying with Dobson, or whether he found out nothing at all, would make little difference. Either way, he'd cut a path to Dobson's.

Even with Delbert out of town, she wondered how much damage McReedy would cause. She pushed her horse into a gallop.

In the front yard, Jessie slowed her horse to a walk, then smounted outside the barn. She didn't seen any sign of McReedy; perhaps his horse was already in the stable.

She entered the barn and still saw no sign of McReedy's mount. She had an odd feeling about this. Where was Chase? And come to think of it, where was the stable boy?

Jessie had opened the gate to her stall when suddenly a powerful arm reached out and grabbed her around the waist. She was about to scream when a meaty hand clamped itself over her mouth.

Jessie struggled fiercely, but in vain. The man was too strong. Her elbow jabs had little effect; her kicking legs couldn't find the man's shins. She had one other hope. Jessie snapped her mouth down hard on the man's hand. She thought she caught the inside of his palm between her teeth. . . . Abruptly, everything went black.

* * *

In the saloon, McReedy had overheard two men talking about the blond woman Dobson was hiding up at his place. McReedy didn't wait around; he knew they were talking about Jessie.

He had asked a man on the street for directions, then left immediately for the Dobson house.

But he reined in on a small knoll overlooking the house. He realized he couldn't very well go barging right up to the door and demand to see Jessie. Even though the men in the saloon had used the word "hiding," Chase couldn't be sure Jessie wasn't there of her own free will. He didn't doubt for a minute that Jessie would take the bit between her teeth and go striding right up to Dobson. But there was also the slim possibility that Jessie was being held there against her wishes. If she was in trouble, he had to do something, but if she was all right, how would he explain his presence?

Chase decided it was best to study the house awhile to see if he could catch anything suspicious going on. He wished he had a pair of field glasses; he was rather far away, but he dared not go any closer for fear of being spotted.

The hours passed as he lazily observed the house. He saw no sign of Dobson or Jessie. Chase decided that if nothing turned up come nightfall, he would steal down to the house and have a closer look. But his impatience was getting the best of him, and he was considering another plan when he saw the rider pull in at the barn. Even from this distance there was no mistaking Jessie's statuesque form.

McReedy stuck his head into the barn. "Jessie?" he said softly. There was no answer. He walked across to the house.

He knocked loudly on the front door. A moment later a Spanish woman opened it.

"I'm looking for Jessica Starbuck," Chase said as he removed his dusty hat.

Before the servant could answer, a woman's voice called out from the parlor. "Who is it, Juanita?"

"I'm looking for Jessie," Chase repeated, loud enough for the woman to hear.

A moment later, Sylvia appeared at the door. She studied him coldly. "And who are you?" she demanded to know.

"My name's Chase, Chase Starbuck. I'm her brother," he said confidently.

"I didn't know she had a brother."

McReedy tried to stay calm. He reminded himself there was no reason for this woman to know anything about Jessie's family. Chase himself didn't know if Jessie had any brothers, and he was a darned sight more intimate with Jessie than this woman was. Just because she didn't know there was a brother didn't mean that there couldn't be one.

Chase shrugged. "She does and I'm him," he said with a friendly smile.

"I'm afraid she's not in right now. She's gone riding and I don't know when she'll be back."

"I thought I saw her ride into the yard."

"That so?" Sylvia said with surprise.

McReedy nodded. "I was coming across from that hill," he said pointing. "I tried hollerin' but I don't think she heard me."

"Are you sure it was her?"

"A man knows his own sister," he said with a polite smile.

"I'll go see if she's in her room. Why don't you come in, Mr. Starbuck?"

"Call me Chase."

"Very well." Sylvia smiled. "I'm Sylvia, Delbert Dobson's daughter."

"Pleased to meet you, ma'am," he said as he bowed from the waist.

"You'll be more comfortable in the parlor," she said sweetly. "This way..."

Chase followed her into the lushly appointed room, where he lowered his frame into a deeply padded leather chair.

"I'll be right back," Sylvia said as she closed the door behind her.

She rushed up the stairs to Jessie's room. She knocked softly, then opened the door. The room was empty.

Quietly, she went down the back stairs and out the kitchen door.

She walked quickly to the barn, saw that it too was empty, then walked around to the rear of the building.

Colligan was there, hitching up the buckboard. He smiled when he saw her.

"It's all taken care of," he said proudly. He nodded towards a burlap-covered pile in the back of the wagon.

"That's her?" Sylvia asked.

Colligan nodded. "Nailed her as she walked into the barn." Sylvia went pale. "Don't worry, she ain't dead," Colligan assured her. "What fun would that be?" he said with an ugly grin. "She's just out cold."

"We've got problems," she said simply.

Colligan eyed her suspiciously. "You changin' yer mind?"

Sylvia ignored the question. "Her brother's in the house. He wants to see her."

He seemed unconcerned. "Tell him she ain't here."

"He saw her ride up."

168

"What'll you do?" he asked dumbly.

"What will *you* do?" she demanded. "He knows she's here. If he doesn't find her, he'll track her down. He looks like the type that won't give up."

"A tough hombre, huh?"

"Not too tough, but tough enough to cause you trouble if you don't take care of him now."

Colligan was clearly thinking it over.

Sylvia continued. "He'll keep looking until he finds his sister—or you," she added menacingly.

Colligan's jaw set. "Where is he?"

"In the parlor."

"Might just as well take care of it now as later. Tell him his sister's in the barn. I'll be waiting for him."

Sylvia shook her head. "It'll look suspicious. Why wouldn't she come back to the house?"

"How the hell do I know?" he snapped, his brain clearly overworked.

"You better go in and get him. I'll finish harnessing the wagon." He didn't move at first. "Go on," she said sharply. "It'll be as easy as the woman was. He won't be expecting anything."

"All right. Wait here," he said. "And have some rope ready."

The door opened.

McReedy stood up. "Jessie—"

The first thing he noticed was that it was not Jessie. The second thing he noticed was the Colt revolver pointed straight at him.

Colligan stepped into the room and closed the door behind him.

"Where's Jessie?" McReedy demanded. "What's happened to her?"

"Unhook that gunbelt and let it drop."

"Where is she?" McReedy repeated.

"You don't do as I say, and you'll never find out," Colligan sneered.

"If anything has happened to her..."

"Mister, you don't drop that gunbelt now, you won't live another minute."

McReedy did as he was told.

Colligan moved around behind him. "We're going to take a walk out to the barn. I'll be right behind you. You try and make a break for it and you won't get more'n five feet. Now move." He jabbed McReedy with the gun.

As they walked through the house, the gun remained pressed into McReedy's back. But once outside, Colligan backed off some. "I'm right behind you," Colligan reminded his prisoner.

Despite the warning, McReedy looked for any chance of escape. Colligan sensed that. "Make yer move. I could use the target practice," he growled. Then he let out a dry chuckle. "Think you'll have any better luck than them rabbits? You're a damned sight bigger and a hell of a lot slower, but you're welcome to take yer chances."

"Once I find Jessie, I may try my luck," McReedy promised.

"I'm lookin' forward to it," Colligan replied. "Now get around back," he instructed as they came to the barn.

McReedy was surprised to see Sylvia, but not totally. He suspected she was the one who had called in the plug-ugly, but he didn't expect to find her waiting there for him. He looked her straight in the eye. "If anything has happened to her, I'll be back for you, too."

"Shut up," Colligan growled. He turned to Sylvia. "Tie his hands behind him, then his feet."

When she finished he went over to check the knots. "Good job," he said dryly. "Now up in the wagon."

"My feet are tied," McReedy protested.

Roughly, Colligan ripped the bandanna from around McReedy's neck, then used it to gag his prisoner. "You talk too much an' get on my nerves," he said by way of an explanation. "Now get into that wagon bed. Hop, like a rabbit." He laughed at his own joke, but the gun remained steady.

McReedy hopped over to the buckboard. Then, not so gently, he was pushed into the back. Colligan lifted the burlap cover, exposing for a moment the unconscious body of Jessie. "Find what you're looking for, fella?" he said with a nasty laugh. Then he brought the butt of his gun down hard on the back of McReedy's neck.

Chapter 16

Ki pulled the buggy around to the back door, then walked into the kitchen. Juanita was surprised and pleased to see him.

"Dobson sent me home ahead," Ki explained. "He'll return tomorrow, by stage."

"I am glad. It has been dull without you," she said with a twinkle in her eye.

"How has Sylvia been behaving?" he asked casually.

Juanita shrugged. "The *señora* is the *señora*. Always the same."

"No trouble, then?"

"No, not really."

Ki could see her hesitation. "You don't seem positive. What has happened?"

"I am not sure. Yesterday, a man came. The *señorita's* brother—*señorita* Jessie."

"What?" Ki exclaimed.

"Her brother came looking for her."

172

"Her brother?" Ki repeated. Juanita nodded. He held back the rest of his questions until she finished her story.

"Yes," she continued. "He was waiting in the parlor. Then I saw a man, a man I did not know, lead him out to the barn. He had a gun pointed at his back."

"What did Jessie say about it?"

"I have not told her," Juanita said. "I have not seen her," she added quickly.

Ki resisted the impulse to run up the stairs to Jessie's room. If she were in the house, Juanita would know. Instead, he delved for more information. "Her brother, what did he look like?"

"He was tall, about your height," she began. Then, after a moment's thought, she shrugged. "It is hard for me to remember. . . ."

It always amazed Ki how unobservant most people were. He knew it was useless to press for a better description. "What was his name?" he asked instead.

Juanita seemed confused by the question. "It was her brother; his name was Starbuck, of course. . . ." Then she realized Ki wanted to know the man's Christian name. "I think it was Chase."

"Thank you, Juanita."

Ki rushed to the barn. Jessie's horse was in its stall. Since Juanita had not seen Jessie, Ki assumed she was out. But her horse was in. Either she had come back recently, or. . .

He grabbed the stable hand. "When did that horse come in?" he demanded.

The hand shrugged. "Sometime yesterday, I reckon."

"When yesterday?"

"I don't know. I was out walking Sultan around the lake. When I came back the horse was grazing in the yard."

"Why did you go up to the lake?"

"Miss Sylvia asked me to."

"Does she ask you to do that often?"

"First time."

Ki ran back to the house. He went straight to Sylvia's room, knocked on the door, and without waiting threw it open.

"Where is Jessie?" he asked in a calm but threatening voice.

Sylvia, who was sitting in a chair by the window, looked up from her book.

"How dare you barge in here like that?" she said sharply.

Ki moved closer, towering above her. "Where is she?" he repeated. His eyes were burning coals, seething with anger.

Sylvia realized it would not be wise to defy him. "I do not know," she said with an innocent smile.

"Where is her brother?"

"I imagine they are together."

"A man took him out of this house at gunpoint," Ki informed her.

"That seems highly unbelievable."

"Who was that man?"

"How would I possibly know?"

"I am not amused." His voice cut like a knife. He grabbed Sylvia roughly by the shoulders. "If anything has happened to Jessie, I'll . . ."

"You'll what?" she said contemptuously. "Hit me, rape me?"

That gave Ki an idea. "That won't be necessary. I'll simply bring Juanita to the marshall's office in Helena, where she can file charges against you for attempted murder."

"Hah! No one would believe you."

"There's the gouge in the study floor, and the bullet that I dug out of it. A derringer takes a uniquely small cartridge...."

"You don't scare me," Sylvia hissed.

"They might be interested in knowing why you tried to kill Juanita."

"And that, no one will ever know," she said triumphantly.

"Are you sure?" Ki said wickedly.

Sylvia studied Ki closely, then chose her words carefully. "First, no one would believe you."

"Your father might."

Sylvia's body tensed, and her face became pale, but her voice stayed steady. "And secondly, and more importantly, if they knew what you were doing to me before Juanita walked in, they'd kill you."

"I am not afraid to die," Ki answered simply.

Sylvia became frightened. Not only because Ki might expose their act of sex, but because she suddenly realized that Ki had something he could hold over her head forever. To keep the truth from being revealed she would always have to give in to his demands. As long as he lived she would be at his mercy. And that gave her another idea.

"I do recall a man calling on Father, earlier yesterday," she said earnestly.

"What is his name?"

"I don't know. I think he's a local horse trader."

Ki pulled her to her feet. "Take me to him."

"I'm not sure where he lives."

"You'll find him," Ki said confidently.

She would indeed. Ki had become a dangerous man, and there was one way to take care of dangerous men. Colligan would make smooth work of it.

The pounding in her head slowly brought Jessie back to consciousness. She opened her eyes but was unable to focus clearly; the room was a blur. She tried to sit up but couldn't. The pain was sharp, but that wasn't what kept her from her goal. She realized with a start that her arms and legs were tied down.

Her vision cleared and she saw that she was tied spread-eagled to a metal cot. She turned her head to see more of the room, and gasped. A few feet from her, McReedy was tied to a chair. He was gagged but his eyes lit up when he saw her move.

Jessie tried to remember how she got here. The ramshackle cabin they were in held no clue. The last memory Jessie had was of walking into the barn.

Outside, she heard a horse approach. Chase's eyes moved quickly. He was trying to warn her. It was a wise idea to play possum; she closed her eyes.

The door banged open, and heavy, uneven footsteps clomped on the floorboards. The stink of filth and liquor filled the room. Carefully, Jessie cracked open one eye. Through a narrow slit which was hidden by her eyelashes, she saw the man who had accosted her in the dining room —Colligan. She shut her eye.

He moved closer; she could feel his breath on her face. "Still out cold," he muttered to himself.

Colligan grabbed a chair and dragged it to the side of the cot. "I don't usually hit women," he said as he slumped into the chair. "But the bitch bit my hand. Drew blood at that!"

He pulled a knife from his belt. McReedy's eyes opened wide. Colligan smiled. "I ain't gonna cut her throat," he assured McReedy. "But maybe you'll be wishin' I had, when you see what I'm a-gonna do to her," he said, and let out a nasty laugh.

McReedy struggled frantically with his bonds, his chair rattling from the effort. Colligan leaped at his captive and thrust the knife in his face. "I ain't got much use for you," he snarled. "You cause too much trouble, an' I'll slit yer throat wide open."

McReedy settled down.

"That's better," Colligan said. Then he returned to his chair. He stared down at Jessie, then brought the knife to her neck. "When you wake, little lady, you're gonna be in for one hell of a surprise."

Jessie felt the point of the blade resting lightly against her skin. She tried to remain calm and keep from flinching.

She felt the knife slowly make its way along her collar-bone. There was no pressure on the blade, and it moved without cutting. But that could change at any moment.

"I'm real disappointed you ain't feeling better, ma'am," Colligan began. "I did think you'd be more chipper by today," he continued to ramble. "Had me a good bottle of whiskey, an' I sure am in the mood right now. But it ain't gonna be much fun if you ain't fightin' any."

Jessie took that as her cue. As long as she could fake being unconscious, she could forestall the inevitable. What she would do with her borrowed time, she did not yet know. But every minute was precious. Given time there might be a way out, yet. She would not abandon hope.

The knife reached the first button of Jessie's shirt. With a quick flick, the button popped off. Colligan smiled and, using the knife, pushed open her blouse as he slid the blade down to the next button. That one too came off easily.

When the third button was removed, Jessie's soft, white breasts became fully exposed.

"You think I'm a fool, hey, big brother? Maybe. An'

177

maybe I should take her now. Long as she's still warm, I know I'll have me a good time."

He pushed aside her shirt so he could view her pink nipples. Then, without warning, he quickly slapped the flat of the blade down on her breast.

Though it surprised Jessie, she didn't cry out or open her eyes. She couldn't control all of her body's reactions, though. The cold metal of the blade caused her nipple to harden.

Seeing her rosy bud stiffen and protrude only excited Colligan more. Methodically, he circled the nipple with the tip of his blade. "That just about decides it," he said to no one in particular. "I can have her any time I damn well please. As often as I please, too."

Colligan stood up. Jessie could hear him undoing his belt buckle. A cold shiver ran up her spine.

"Things are sure different than the first time we met," he said with a thick, dry voice. "Seems like I owe you a lesson or two in manners, ma'am. And the learnin' begins now!"

Ki rode close to Sylvia, keeping a watchful eye on her. He wouldn't put it past her to try something stupid. She had started out acting unsure and indecisive; but now she seemed to know exactly where she was taking Ki. Ki interpreted that as nothing more than a silly ploy. Despite everything she had said, Ki had little doubt that she was somehow responsible for the recent turn of events. If she was leading him to Jessie, it was only because she felt it was in her best interests to do so.

Ki realized he might be riding straight into a trap. But if this was the quickest way of getting to Jessie, he would risk it.

"Over that hill there's a small cabin," Sylvia said after an hour of riding due west. "I think that's where he lives."

"Lead the way," Ki answered.

"But I . . ."

Ki smiled to himself. She obviously expected a trap, and didn't wish to be the one caught in the middle.

"I thought you'd let me go home now," Sylvia continued nervously.

"How do I know that's the man I'm looking for?"

"I'm sure it is," she answered quickly.

"In that case I definitely need you."

"Why?"

"To exchange for Jessie and her brother," he answered simply.

"I don't know that they're here; I don't even know that Colligan took them," she said hastily.

"Colligan?"

"I think that's the horse trader's name. . . ." Sylvia said innocently.

"I know the man," Ki remarked dryly. "He's no horse trader."

Sylvia looked frightened. She tried to swing her horse around, but Ki quickly reached forward and grabbed the animal's bit.

"If Colligan is down there, and he has Jessie, you will have suddenly outlived your usefulness," he said menacingly. Ki spoke his words slowly; the threat was all the worse for it.

Sylvia started her horse towards the hill, but she remained defiant. "What makes you think she's still alive?" she said maliciously.

Ki did not answer.

It was a tense ride to the cabin. The field they had to cross was less than fifty yards wide, but Ki half expected a rifle to open up fire at any moment. Ten yards from the cabin he stopped his horse.

"You too," he instructed Sylvia as he dismounted.

This was the chance she was waiting for. She started to swing down from the saddle, but never did. As soon as her first foot touched the ground, she let out a loud yell: "Colligan!" Then she quickly hopped back onto her horse and spurred it into a gallop. She gave another yell as she sped off.

Ki was unconcerned. Her yell confirmed that this was Colligan's cabin. She really was no more use to him. If he needed her later he knew where to find her.

He turned his attention to the cabin.

Colligan had just removed his gunbelt and was starting to unbutton his pants when he heard the shout.

"Damn! That woman won't give me a minute's peace," he grumbled as he went to the door.

He stepped outside. "You!" he said in surprise as he spotted Ki. "I don't know what you've come around here for," he said with a grin, "but I'm gonna beat the stuffin's out of you." With that he rushed at Ki.

Colligan no doubt expected an easy fight. Perhaps even another one-punch knockout.

Therefore, he was stunned when Ki's foot smacked into his chest. He was even more astonished to find himself knocked on his ass.

He rose quickly and rushed at Ki. Ki held his ground and waited. When he saw Colligan's fat fist lash out, he ducked down and delivered two hard jabs to the man's gut.

Colligan swung around with his other fist. Ki blocked it with his forearm, then connected with a punch to his opponent's face. Colligan's lip split open, but he seemed impervious to the pain. He again rushed at Ki.

This time Ki stepped back, giving himself enough leg-room to deliver a solid *mae-geri-keage*. The kick snapped hard into Colligan's face, and the man reeled back. Ki followed that up with a quick roundhouse kick to the side of the head, and Colligan staggered.

That gave Ki a moment to think. Chances were good that Jessie was in the cabin. But there was always the slim possibility that Colligan had her hidden away somewhere. Ki couldn't take the gamble; not with Jessie's life. He had to be careful to keep Colligan alive.

Colligan had shaken off the effects of the kicks, and was coming back for more. Ki watched for the punch, and was slightly surprised when the man closed quickly and tried to grab him in a bearhug.

Ki took Colligan's own momentum and turned it against his opponent. The smoothly executed *semo-otoshi,* or shoulder throw, slammed Colligan flat on his back. He lay there, dazed and confused.

McReedy heard what he took to be the sounds of a fight. Taking the chair with him, he tried to stand up and walk over to the cot. There he hoped to maneuver himself into a position where he could untie Jessie's ropes. But after two steps, he fell crashing to the floor. He tried to struggle back to his feet, but the chair he was tied to made it difficult. He crawled to the corner to see if he could use the leverage of the wall to help him.

Jessie too heard the struggle outside. She realized this might be her one chance to call for help. She hesitated, weighing the options. She didn't know who Colligan was fighting. There was a chance her would-be rescuer was as bad as her captor. And if she called out, Colligan would know she was no longer unconscious. Though those were both risks she was willing to take, there was the other possibility that, given enough time, Chase would be able to free her.

She decided to wait a few minutes to see if Chase could regain his feet.

Ki stood over Colligan. "Tell me where Jessie is and you'll live."

For an answer Colligan brought his leg up into Ki's back. Ki, thinking the man was spent, was caught off guard, and went stumbling forward.

Colligan sprang to his feet and, bending over, pulled a small dagger from his boot.

Ki turned in time to see the man, and the weapon, come at him.

"I'm gonna slice that coolie throat of yours," Colligan promised as he slashed wildly with the dagger.

Though it was a small knife, Ki had no doubt that it could easily cut his throat. He would have to show caution.

Colligan lunged. Ki side stepped, grabbed the man's wrist, and, with a loud shout, brought the heel of his hand down on the man's forearm. Something had to give. Usually it was the bone in the arm. It was a fast, effective way of separating a knife from a hand. This time, though, Colligan's wrist was so large that before the bone cracked the wrist slipped out of Ki's grasp.

Jessie smiled. She would recognize that cry anywhere. There was not a man alive that had a *kiai*, a spirit yell, like Ki's. She took a deep breath and opened her mouth. . . .

Ki pulled a *shuriken* from his vest pocket and held it between his knuckles. He would not bother again with trying to break the man's arm. The next time Colligan attacked, he would come away with a slashed forearm. It

182

was near impossible to wield a knife when the tendons in the wrist were severed.

Colligan stepped forward.

Ki waited. Colligan lunged. Then Ki heard it. "Ki!" There was no mistaking the voice.

Ki reacted instantly, and abandoned his original plan. For a brief moment, he ignored Colligan's knife, and stepped forward into his opponent. That took Colligan by surprise. He didn't expect an unarmed opponent to advance on him. It was the last surprise of his life.

Ki lashed out with his fist, his hand whipping across Colligan's throat.

Colligan barely felt the blow. But blood gushed out of his jugular and poured down onto his throat.

A second later he fell over—dead.

Jessie, Ki, and McReedy confronted Dobson in the parlor. They had just begun to talk when Sylvia burst into the room.

"Don't believe anything they have to say, Father," she said frantically. "They're trying to deceive you. They all know each other, they're all in this together. They came here to cheat you, to steal our money. . . ."

Jessie ignored her and continued: "As I was saying, Delbert, I have enough proof to send you to prison—"

"She's lying," Sylvia snapped.

Jessie shook her head. "I have the ledger from your Greenville office."

"And I overheard your conversation with Williams," Ki added.

"Can't you see they're lying?" Sylvia pleaded again.

Jessie now turned to Sylvia. "And I can get you on conspiracy to commit murder."

183

Sylvia let out a haughty laugh.

"Colligan confessed everything to save his own skin," Jessie said confidently. Sylvia had no idea that Colligan was far beyond confessing anything.

For the first time Dobson seemed scared. "Is that true?" he asked his daughter.

Sylvia shook her head, but there was no denying the fear in her eyes. It was obvious that she was the one lying.

"You can't fight it, Delbert. I have as many lawyers as you, and I have all the proof."

Dobson barely heard her. Shocked, he stared at his daughter.

"A scandal will disgrace your whole family," Jessie said softly.

Delbert slowly turned to Jessie. "Let her go, and I'll confess to everything."

Jessie at first said nothing.

"I'll draw up the papers in my study. Whatever land I took will go back to the rightful owners."

Jessie nodded.

Dobson turned to leave, then paused in front of his daughter to caress her tear-streaked cheek. Jessie started to follow him out. "Please, Jessie," Dobson said weakly. "If you wouldn't mind, I'd like a few minutes by myself."

"I understand," she said.

But she didn't.

Minutes later they heard a single shot come from behind the closed door of the study.

Delbert Dobson was never to become governor. Slumped over his desk, he lay in a pool of his own blood. The gun, still smoking, lay in his lifeless hand.

"He wasn't an evil man," Jessie said with much regret.

Ki and McReedy remained respectfully silent.

"Let's go home," Jessie said softly, and turned for the door.

Sobbing, Sylvia ran to her father.

Watch for

LONE STAR AND THE JAMES GANG'S LOOT

sixty-fifth novel in the exciting
LONE STAR
series from Jove

coming in January!